# FAIR TRADE

They had Helga, Jaime Henry's woman.

There was the half-breed who moved like a ghost and killed like a devil and called himself Espada, the Ace of Spades.

There was the giant black called Huggo, who had the power in his two huge hands to tear apart anything on two feet.

There was the bestial gunman named Sloane, whose past was littered with men cut down by his bullets and women ravished by his insatiable lusts.

They had Helga—and Jaime Henry tried not to think of what they were doing with her.

He just thought of what he would have in return—

their lives. . . .

*The Latest Blazing Western Adventures*
*From Dell Books*

LAST CALL FOR A GUNFIGHTER *by Bliss Lomax*
MARAUDERS' MOON *by Luke Short*
MAÑ ON THE BLUE *by Luke Short*
BOLD RIDER *by Luke Short*
KING COLT *by Luke Short*
CLAYBURN *by Al Conroy*

*The Stanton Saga by Tom W. Blackburn*

YANQUÍ
RANCHERO
EL SEGUNDO
PATRÓN
COMPAÑEROS

# El Segundo

Tom W. Blackburn

A DELL BOOK

*For Tom III,*
*my Segundo, who has warmed his*
*backside at distant campfires*
*and lived with legend and has*
*the guns to prove it.*

Published by
DELL PUBLISHING CO., INC.
1 Dag Hammarskjold Plaza
New York, N.Y. 10017

ISBN: 0-440-13491-9

Printed in the United States of America
Previous Dell Edition #3491
New Dell Edition
First printing—October 1978

# El Segundo

# CHAPTER 1

Unlike the torpid basins of the eastern seaboard and the humid central valleys of the great American rivers, there are no summer dog days on the high grass. Even with the end of the rains after the passing of the summer solstice and the melting of the last of the snow on the high peaks, when the sun hangs high and the grass browns dry and cures on the stem to tinder underfoot, the air remains cool. But the earth heats. So does a man in the unshaded open.

Jaime Henry came down the dry wash, hazing half a dozen dusty longhorn steers whose castrated state did not lessen their native cussedness. They had worked themselves three or four miles up the wash to a steep-sided cutbank box at its head, from which they could not climb, and they were just too damned ornery to sensibly turn tail back the way they had come. They had been trapped there two or three days without graze or water and would have died in a few more if he had not come upon them and seen their predicament.

But out of characteristic sheer perversity, they had given him hell all of the way back down. His horse's coat was dark-patched with sweat turned to mud by the heavy dust they kicked up in his face. So was his shirt where it was plastered to him. His mouth was gritted with the taste of dust as well.

He had them within a couple of hundred yards and plain sight of the meandering run of the Cimarroncito before they threw up their heads as though scenting the water for the first time and went galloping off clumsily toward it, tails high, like the discovery was theirs alone. He pulled up, wearily hooking a knee over the horn of his saddle, and exasperatedly relieved himself of some of his choicest Missouri profanity.

The romance of cow-nursing: there were some days bullshit was more like it. It was one thing to be Spencer Stanton's foreman, *segundo* on the Corona and responsible in the boss's absence for more than a quarter of a million acres of the best rangeland in New Mexico and lord only knew now just how many thousand head of obstinate beefsteak on the hoof. It was quite another to hammer your butt to your navel for two hours to chouse a few strays out of a trap you knew damned well they'd gotten themselves into on purpose. There just had to be a better way for a grown man in his right mind to spend the shag end of a hot afternoon.

The steers splashed into the creek and watered, then moved unconcernedly on down the stream to join the bunch of forty or fifty from which they had strayed in the first place. Muzzles down to the grass, tails switching at the wicked bite of an occasional deerfly or overly ambitious mosquito, they lost themselves in the anonymity of the placidly grazing little herd.

Without changing position in the saddle, Jaime let his horse move on down to the meandering stream, the sound of the water as welcome as the sight. He dismounted, loosed the cinch, and let the animal water. Pulling a couple of tufts of bank-grass, he rubbed the wet coat of the horse down enough to suit his conscience and then sauntered a few yards upstream.

The Cimarroncito swung around a bend there and had cut itself a little pool floored with clean sand under the bank. He saw the darting shadow of a trout as his own shadow fell upon the water. It was too inviting to resist. He peeled off his clothes and jumped in. The chill was welcome and he splashed about, sloshing the dust and heat from his body. Thinking of the sorry, dust-laden state of his clothing, he returned for it and rinsed each garment out thoroughly as well.

Climbing out, he crossed a little patch of grass, yet green and nearly as thick and smooth as a tended lawn, to a clump of willows. He spread his clothes on these to dry and went back to the patch of grass, sprawling luxuriantly onto his back there. After a few minutes, out of respect for the unexposed whiteness of the usually covered portions of his body and how fast the sun could burn untanned skin in this high air, he rolled over. It was only then that he saw the other horse and its rider beside another willow clump no more than a dozen yards away.

He instinctively started to scramble up, then realized his clothes were too far away and flopped defensively onto his belly again. He had no idea how long the girl in the saddle had been watching him. Long enough, he supposed, and so his flopping attempt at modesty was probably sufficiently ludicrous under the circumstances, but her burst of laughter angered him.

"God damn it," he yelled with his nose in the grass, "don't just sit there. Fetch me my pants."

He heard saddle leather creak as she stepped down and the whisper of her Ute half-boots as she crossed the grass to his improvised clothesline. She came back and dropped some of the garments beside him. He clutched them to him and came awkwardly to his knees. She stood a few feet away, her back turned primly to him. But her shoulders were still shaking. He stood up and angrily jerked on his summer half-drawers and his pants.

"That was a hell of a thing to do!" he growled as he buttoned up the fly.

Helga Cagle turned back to him then.

"I'm sorry, Jaime," she said. "Honest. I saw you coming down that draw with those strays and I cut over this way to meet you. I didn't realize what you were doing here until too late. Then you seemed to be enjoying yourself so much I didn't want to startle you."

She was sober and earnest enough, but her eyes were dancing and he knew she was not all that contrite.

"Now I know why you ride out from the house every time you get a chance," he accused. "How many of the hands have you caught like this?"

"You're the first," she grinned. "They're more modest."

Folding her skirt properly beneath her, she sank cross-legged to the grass at his feet and invitingly patted a place beside her.

"Simmer down. It's all in the family. Your socks and shirt are still too wet to put on and there's a lot of sun yet. We might as well wait a bit."

Jaime sat down but could not yet find words fit for feminine ears. Helga tossed her heavy, sun-glinted golden braids over her shoulders and her mischievous, deep blue, almost violet eyes ran over his naked torso with frank interest.

"You know, you're a better figure of a man than I would have thought, seeing you around the house all this time with your shirt on," she said critically.

"Let me pick the time and place and I'd have showed you a hell of a long time before now," he grumbled.

"Brag, brag," she chided. "Come to think of it, you look kind of funny. Patchy. Like a piebald pinto."

Jaime knew what she meant. His hands and wrists to the cuffline of his shirt, and his face, throat, and chest from the sweatband line of his hat to the vee usually exposed by the open collar and two or three additional buttons of his shirt, were tanned to the deep mahogany of polished leather. All else, above and below, was faintly blue-veined and milk-white. Her continuing regard disturbed him as much as had her laughter. But for entirely different reasons.

She braced her arms back a little, palms to the sod, and leaned against them. The movement tightened the bodice of the simple, square-cut, Indian-style shift which was the usual feminine summer attire on the Corona and which 'Mana Stanton taught her to make when she came out of the malpais and became a part of the ranch household. The thin, taut material revealingly outlined her slender figure and magnificent breasts, nipples outthrust in tantalizing relief.

He realized that the pose was not conscious and that she was unaware of the sudden turmoil in him, but he could not help remembering. He remembered that he had once kissed this girl on the banks of the big Cimarron where it came down from the mountains and the old summer camps of the Utes. That had been in her first months on the Corona, after 'Mana Stanton had become pregnant with young Tito and Spence Stanton had agreed to let this mistreated and abandoned waif he had rescued on the malpais stay on and help in the house.

The kiss had been an unexpected thing. A sudden uncontrollable impulse. And without her leave. Yet she had let him press her back against the grass for one long, earth-shaking moment. Then she had calmly put the nails of both hands to his cheeks and raked down so hard that he had had to grow a beard to hide the marks until they had healed. He remembered the kiss and would have forgotten the marks for another. But it was an issue he did not press. He had learned many things on the long way out from his cracker birthplace in the rank Missouri hills, but never how to beg.

He had held his peace, thereafter, but his eyes were seldom far from her when she was about. If she was ever aware, she gave no sign that he could read.

He remembered, too, a night a few months later. He had seen late lamplight in a window of Spence Stanton's uncurtained office and he had gone up to the house to have a showdown with Spence over this girl.

Meaning to knock on the lighted window, he stepped close and saw this slender, rounded figure now smiling teasingly across at him standing proudly in all her young, long-limbed, stark-naked glory in the lamplight and fireglow on the hearth before Spence Stanton.

Stumbling blindly back to the corrals, he had saddled up and ridden the night out, raging in the belief that the master of the Corona, his mentor and more than a father to him, was using this pale, rosy flesh, young enough to be his daughter, for pleasure while his own wife was heavy with child. It had taken the most merciless beating any man had ever handed Jaime Henry for Spence to convince him that what he had seen was only the result of a distraught and friendless young girl's temporarily imagined infatuation with an older man to whom she believed she owed her life and the roof over her head.

Spence had admitted to the same temptation that had surged furiously through Jaime at sight of that soft-lit figure on the boss's hearth. But he had not touched her. He had instead made her put her shift back on and had set her straight and sent her back to bed. Jaime did not know, even now, what Spencer Stanton told her that night, but from then on she seemed to understand. There was only one woman in the boss's life. There was only one woman on the Corona. That was 'Mana Stanton.

If there had been sadness in Helga at her rejection, she recovered swiftly. Or it did not show. Not then and not since. It did not now.

"There's some other things funny about you," she said suddenly, breaking the silence of Jaime's remembering.

"Let 'em go," he told her. "You've had your laugh for the day."

"Oh, don't be a sorehead," she protested good-naturedly. "You don't talk much."

"Some things I'd rather think."

"Like now?"

He nodded. "Got a notion it keeps me out of a lot of trouble."

"Maybe," she agreed. "Maybe it does. And that name. Who ever heard of a Mexican with a river-town accent?"

"Spence started that. When he picked me up in Santa Fe when I was sixteen. For Jim. That's what I was born with."

"Jaime. I wonder why?"

"I don't know."

"I think I do," Helga said thoughtfully. "I had a long talk with him one night. He told me a lot of things. He was married before."

Jaime nodded.

"Had a family," Helga continued. "Back east somewhere. Two boys. One was named Jimmy. I don't think he likes to remember."

"What suits him suits me."

"Jaime—" she was speaking to him, now, not of his name. She straightened her crossed legs out before her and leaned back a little more on her braced hands. If she had not been conscious of her body before, she was now. "Tell me what you're thinking."

He looked at her a long moment, the thoughts she wanted rushing over him.

"If I can do it in my own way."

He crossed to her on his knees and she lay back before him on the grass. Her hands were warmer than the sun upon his bare back as she opened her lips to his. And she kissed him as hungrily and honestly as he did her. They broke and he came back insistently. Her mouth welcomed him eagerly and her arms tightened about him. When he found and tugged down the shoulder of her shift, she let him cup and lift her breast with a little tremor of anticipation.

The wind roared in his ears and they rocked each other. So long to wait but so much to wait for. All he had dreamed about her had been true. This was no night-tossing fantasy of his mind. This was a woman fit for a man. Young and beautiful and giving. For real. But as their urgency grew and he would have touched her elsewhere, she caught his hand and drew it back to her breast, holding it clasped there.

"No, Jaime," she murmured. "Understand and let it go at that."

He reluctantly lay back beside her, trying to do just that, but he could not. She turned toward him presently as his breathing eased. Her hand was cool against the back of his neck and her fingers crept gently into his hair.

"It was the manness I suddenly had to have," she continued after a little. "But I'm not sure of you, Jaime. I'm not sure of me. And I have to be."

His own loneliness and the deep, dark, lusting current of his desire for this girl surged achingly through Jaime Henry, but he would not force a man beyond his conscience in anything and he could not a woman, so he remained motionless and silent in acquiescence.

They lay there quietly in each other's arms while the sun slanted down at them and his clothing slowly dried. After a long time Helga suddenly raised to an elbow, rolled to him, and pressed her open mouth again to his. Her lips moved, hungering even more voraciously than before. Her body, trembling, writhed insistently against his. Volition deserted them both. But only for an instant. Just as suddenly as she had bent over him, Helga sat up and calmly tugged up the shoulder of her dress so that she was completely covered again.

"Stage day," she said. "I've got to get back and give 'Mana a hand if there's any aboard to be fed."

She rose lightly, reached down a hand, and pulled Jamie up. He crossed gingerly on bare feet to the willows and put on socks and boots and shirt and hat. She had caught up his horse and was holding it with her own when he returned. They mounted. Features unsmiling, she looked across at him, her great, luminous eyes unreadable.

"Thank you, Jaime," she said. "You really are a better man than I had any right to expect."

It was small enough reward, he supposed, but he was content. Time was plentiful in this country. There would be other days.

She turned her horse toward the Corona headquarters. He spurred after her and they rode side by side in silence across the shadows beginning to lengthen out from the mountains.

# CHAPTER 2

Occasionally, toward the end of a long day, Romana Ruíz Stanton found herself longing, half in earnest, for a return to the simplicity of earlier times on the Corona. It was not weariness. She was not yet thirty-five. She had been born on this grant and the land had made her strong. The pulse and lust of life was high in her. She was as eager for the challenge of each dawning day and as equal to it as she had been in the beginning.

Nor was her pride in what they had built here any less than that of her absent husband. She relished the security and comfort and increasing elegance of the big stone house and the permanence of the little adobe village slowly growing down by the corrals.

She drew deep satisfaction from the multiplying bunches of cattle mottling the unbroken grass which now included Tito's inheritance, the old Peralta rancho at Mora, as well. This was wealth. Even great wealth, as it was reckoned in this time and place.

It was the stuff of dynasty, as she had dreamed as a girl and as her father and grandfathers had before her since the long ago time the viceroy of a Spanish king had granted the original Corona to them. This she and Spence had accomplished when all before them had failed. It was a land which broke lesser men, even those who had been born and lived and died upon it.

And there was Roberto—Robertito to the village women—Tito to his darker-skinned playmates among the adobes. Nearly five, now. Body hard and healthy and already a competent horseman. Jaime had seen to that, almost from the time he could walk. Giving early promise of filling out in the tall, big-boned, powerful Stanton mold.

Tito, his boy's vocabulary became fluent in three languages—the Mexican Spanish of the land, the *yanqui* English of the new flag flying over the high country, and the curiously musical tongue of the Mountain Utes. This had been her particular vanity, taught to him as she taught Helga, while household chores were afoot.

Their son. This was the ultimate satisfaction. All else was, in the end, for him. To that degree, small as he yet was, he was the Corona and would be long after them.

But as the ranch grew and prospered, there were complexities which had to be faced. Spence was increasingly absent in recent times. Repeatedly in Taos and Santa Fe. Twice in Washington, trying to help organize a civil territorial government to constitutionally replace the military administration which was a carryover from the war. To the military, undermanned and understaffed, all Spanish-speaking New Mexicans were conquered enemies, to be treated as such, although they had not resisted the invasion forces and no battle had been fought with them. And as elsewhere in the States, Indians were Indians, no matter how long they had been upon the land.

There was grave injustice in much of this and much rebellious unrest. There had been the senseless murder of Governor Bent, the most respected trader in the mountain country, and some other army-appointed territorial officials by a disorganized mob at Taos. Father Frederico's old mission church, where 'Mana Stanton herself had once gone to school had been leveled by army howitzers to flush out the insurgents in reprisal. Navajos had raided the Rio Grande villages and Colonel Doniphan had marched into their stronghold, forcing them to a treaty.

Spence grimly reported these affairs had only hardened the army's sense of duty and determination and so accomplished nothing. The task facing him and other men of good will had been made more difficult. He wrote that Sol Wetzel, in whose trading firm the Corona had been a minor partner, had kept a year's count. Nine thousand men, three thousand wagons, twenty-eight thousand oxen, and six thousand California mules had moved more than thirty thousand tons of trade goods and freight into and out of Santa Fe in that time.

A swelling river of commerce flowed down the Trail to Santa Fe from the Missouri river-towns. It flowed past the Corona, little more than thirty miles to the east, almost visible from the window where 'Mana Stanton stood. It was this the army was determined to protect. Hundreds of thousands of *yanqui* dollars in profit.

Justice and a fair participation by all New Mexicans in territorial affairs weighed little enough against that. The military were practical men, whatever uniform they wore or whatever language they spoke. It had always been so.

The tranquility of daily routine lay over the Corona. Jaime, here at the home place, and Abelardo at the Mora ranch saw to that. The appearance of peace lay on the surface over all of the high country. It had for many months now. But Spence was still in Santa Fe, so there was yet need for him there. And his wife was heavy with nameless unease.

'Mana returned her eyes to a plume of dust rising in the south above the Mora trail, now fast becoming a road. The stage—a hardsprung mudwagon actually, to withstand the grueling route it had to travel—but on schedule. One week from Santa Fe to Westport Landing, one week back, two round trips a month.

She had protested mildly when Spence had offered both the Corona and Mora headquarters as relay stations, but he had argued that since the stage traveled straight through, without rest stops except for break-downs or weather, they would be inconvenienced only for an occasional meal. And the contract for relay stock at both stops on the ranch was lucrative enough to make it well worth while. And there was an even greater value, in his opinion. Stock increase on the Corona was now reaching a level which made it prac-tical to begin upgrading on a large scale and market-ing surplus on a regular basis.

It was now time for the Stanton ranch and Stanton beef to become known across the entire length of the Santa Fe Trail in both directions. There was no better way to accomplish this in a newspaperless country than to oblige every commercial traveler to spend a day each way crossing through the heart of the Corona.

Besides, she was too much alone here in his absence. A brief weekly visit with passengers and crews would help relieve the monotony.

She could not tell him then that she thought this was one of the roots of her unease. To her, from the beginning, one of the strengths of the Corona had al-ways been its remoteness and utter self-sufficiency. It seemed to her that whenever others had intruded upon their grass, for whatever reasons, trials and trou-ble had ensued.

She instinctively did not want alien presence on their domain. She did not want the eyes of strangers upon their ambitions here and their dreams. There seemed some spoilation in that. It was not hostility or inhospitality. It was some innate caution, some fore-boding of an unknown but deeply sensed danger.

But in a few weeks, as was so often the case in their life together, she perceived Spence's wisdom if she could not wholly accept it. In spite of herself, she began to anticipate and really look forward to the weekly intrusions. Not often were there passengers of real interest or import. Frequently there were none. The line was too new, the trip too punishing for any but the hardiest. And she had difficulty after so long a period of isolation in making small talk with these men and an occasional woman whom she had not seen before and likely would not again.

But even though the coaches rolled in empty, they rolled. The line was subsidized by a government mail contract. The first in the territory. Spence had helped arrange that. And eastbound out of Santa Fe, there was always word from him when he was absent there.

'Mana noted that the approaching stage had now been seen at the adobes. Crippled old Amelio, the first hand to be hired on the Corona, was on his way up from the corrals with a six-up relay team already in harness, ready to snap to trace-chains in a quick change in the yard. She smiled at a small figure trotting along with the old man, leaning back in two-handed wrangler style on one pair of the trailing ribbons. Since Amelio had taken over this chore with the advent of the stages, Tito had assumed it was his as well and proudly called himself Amelio's *segundo*, expecting a certain amount of respect for the assumption.

She thought the stage was a little early. There was as yet no sign of Helga off toward the draw of the Cimarroncito in the direction in which she had ridden. She was usually prompt in returning from her rides when extra duties were anticipated.

'Mana went below to the kitchen and opened the drafts and shook down the grates of the range in case there was need for hot lids and a warming oven. Freshening the fire was now easily done since they no longer hauled and split firewood from the mountains but burned hard, clean, long-lasting anthracite from the exposed coal seam Raul Archuleta had discovered a few miles up the Vermejo fork. It was surprising how much luxury such small conveniences added to the otherwise changeless workaday household.

She patted out and butter-brushed a dozen rolls from the great pan of riser always under a damp towel on the warming shelf of the stove and slid the big, cast-iron dutch oven of antelope stew forward over hotter lids in case she was to have table guests. If not, supper for themselves would be that much sooner done.

When she sat down at the zinc-topped work table under the kitchen window, she saw that two inbound riders had appeared off toward the Cimarroncito. She smiled again. The rider loping along with Helga Cagle was Jaime Henry.

Not everyone fell in love in a single explosive instant, as she and Spencer Stanton had. Some others were made differently and could not be so fortunate. Sometimes the distances were too great between them for that. Too many remembrances to dismiss at once. Too many uncertainties. Too much restraint. But as she watched the two homeward-bound riders, she thought that one day this circle, too, would close and another strong link would be forged on the Corona. This had long been her hope.

The Santa Fe stage rolled in and bucked to a stop against its brakes in the yard. There was but one passenger, a man riding topside with the driver. He alighted stiffly, was directed, and went around back toward the outhouse. He returned in a few moments and remained standing beside the stage with the driver. Neither man made any move toward the kitchen door.

'Mana did not feel the need for talk and remained where she was. She supposed Abelardo had seen they were especially well fed at the Mora ranch or that they were reluctant to lose time in the hope of avoiding running out of daylight before they reached the next stop at Taylor Springs.

Amelio stepped out the worn team and backed in the fresh spans. Tito moved in quickly and fearlessly but with a due caution which had already become second nature to him around stock and snapped the chains on his side. He stepped back, beaming at Amelio's signal of approval. The driver must have made some comment of approbation as well, for Tito touched the brim of his hat before stepping forward to receive the envelope the man extended to him.

The driver and his passenger stepped to hub and seat. The driver shook out his reins with the yell which for some reason always started a stage team. The coach rolled out on its long way to the distant east of the Missouri. Amelio started back to the corrals with the relieved relay. Only then did Tito turn and run for the house with the envelope in his hand.

He burst in demanding milk, as he usually did at this hour of the day when supper seemed too far distant to bear. She sent him to his stool beside the washstand to wash his hands and dipped a cream-yellow mug for him from the crock. Then she sat down with the envelope, now grimed with the clutch of a small hand.

It was the letter she had come to expect on the stage day whenever Spence was absent. As with all others from him, 'Mana read it rapidly through first, relishing the fine, bold stroke of his hand and the feeling of physical presence it gave her more than the content.

When she had savored this, she read again more slowly, searching out the precise meaning of every word and reading between the lines where she must, for frequently when he was hurried or troubled, he wrote as tersely and economically as he spoke.

She was reading it yet a third time, even more slowly, her brow deep-creased with concern, when Raul Archuleta rode urgently into the yard, leading Jaime's nervously dancing, riderless horse and calling to the *patrona* in alarm that he had met it half a mile below the corrals, coming in from the direction of the Cimarroncito on its own.

They found Jaime by luck and lantern light an hour after dark. He was sprawled in a low swale below the skyline a quarter of a mile downslope from where

'Mana had last seen him riding in with Helga Cagle. He had been shot in the head, his hat neatly vented three or four inches above its snakeskin band. He was unconscious and had not moved, but he was alive.

Some reason prevailed among the Corona crewmen in spite of their uproar of anger and alarm. They sent back for a mattress and a wagon, since the distance was not far.

Sign was hard to read by lantern light and they had been careless in their haste as they rode up. Nevertheless, some tracks were clear. Jaime and Helga had ridden into an ambush of several men. Six or seven, Raul Archuleta thought. His older sons believed there had been more.

Jaime had been shot from the saddle without warning. Probably without seeing or being aware of his assailants. He had gouted a torrent of blood, as some head wounds will, as he fell and lay still.

Helga had made a break for it but had been trapped against a cutbank her horse would not or could not take. Two or three of the ambushers had dismounted there and presumably lashed her in her saddle, for there was no further sign of resistance and her boots had not touched ground. Her horse had accompanied the ambushers when they departed.

It was no casual encounter, but well planned. God only knew how long they had watched and waited for the right opportunity. Their approach as well as their escape route toward the mountains was by a shallow, well-grassed depression below the skyline which would raise no dust and protect them from view in most directions, particularly from the Corona house and the adobe village at the corrals.

It chilled 'Mana to realize that enemies could operate with undiscovered impunity so close to the rancho stronghold. She thought it important that they had shot Jaime deliberately, plainly leaving him for dead, seizing Helga as if she was their sole objective. But it made no sense. And she wanted desperately to find some rationale—some reason—in this so she could know what must be done, since responsibility was now thrust solely upon her.

She paced restlessly before the kitchen range, watching the copper washboiler she had filled steam slowly toward a boil and waiting for the wagon to bring the wounded man in.

# CHAPTER 3

. . . We feel another rebellion is in the making," the open letter on the kitchen table said. A big one. Make or break. But no indication of the form it will take, as yet. Not Indian or native *mexicano*, this time. That much seems sure. Alone, at least.

A sprinkling in the mixture, maybe, along with breeds, Yank opportunists, God knows what other kinds of bastard. Some of the riffraff pouring down the Trail and scattering through the territory these days. A few scoundrels left over from the war.

Every man jack of them itching to get their fingers in our pie here before it's even half baked. The military and their appointees too short-handed and short-sighted to do more than keep trade channels open and damned little else. And nothing we can officially do about it until we can get a civilian government with real self-determination and recognition of our proper place in the union out of Congress . . .

The lamp-lit wagon rolled into the dooryard, most of the village accompanying it. Amelio hobbled into the house ahead of the others and went unbidden up to Tito's room to reassure and stay with him. 'Mana covered the big trestled dining table with blankets. They carried Jaime in from the mattress in the wagon

and placed him there as she directed, where the light
was best.

The room filled with outraged, earnest, anxious
faces. She kept Mama Archuleta with her because she
knew more of this sort of thing than any in the adobes
and sent the rest out. The two women barred the door
against further intrusion and dipped hot water from
the washboiler on the stove and began to bathe
Jaime's wound.

It had bled so copiously and had become so grass-
matted when he fell that it was a gingerly and messy
job, sickening 'Mana with fear the effort might prove
useless. They worked swiftly and silently, each with
their own prayers, cutting away the hair to get at the
wound itself.

> . . . I don't mean to alarm you, *querida*, but I'm
> sending the same orders to Abelardo at the Mora
> ranch. Wetzel and others here are concerned that
> some of us may be moved against personally. To
> force control of our influence, such as it is.
>
> Tell Jaime to be alert for anything out of the or-
> dinary, any unauthorized strangers. Tell him to
> keep all hands within the ranch proper and to
> avoid bunching the crew up for any reason where
> they might be trapped or their effectiveness other-
> wise hampered or destroyed.
>
> Impress the utmost importance of this upon
> him. It may even become necessary to cancel the
> stage contract and close our boundaries to all
> comers until a stable government can be effected
> to control the present chaos. See that Tito remains
> close to the house. Most important, do so yourself.
>
> You have tried to tell me how it would be, but
> it is still difficult for me to realize that as *patrón*
> and *patrona* of the Corona and Mora how utterly
> dependent these people are on us, even here.
> They still look and cling to that kind of influence
> and authority because it springs from the land.

That they understand. That they have faith in. In us, particularly, because we have more land than most.

So I am obliged to remain here a little longer. I am sure you understand I must. Trust Jaime's judgment. He is our *segundo*. I hold him to that . . .

Jaime Henry had never before been a dead man. Damned close a few times, but never quite. It was a dulled but curiously luxuriant feeling, with little sensation. He lay suspended in space, in comfort and without effort. He was alone, with but a single, blinding flash of memory. He was astonished that even that disembodied fragment remained. He had always politely accepted but gravely doubted Father Frederico's frequent, vehement assertions that a new world and eternal life lay over the hill.

He had seen too many men die in too many hard and agonized ways to believe that even the best of them had stepped into any promised land, boots on or off. Or hell, either, for that matter. Most of them had already had all of that they were entitled to when they died.

He had believed that's all there was to it. But damned if there didn't seem to be more, after all. A little, anyway. This lingering shard of recollection. The smash of a bullet into his head and a never completed fall to the ground. No reasons asked and none given. As simple as that.

Then he was aware of something else trying to get to him. Through the hole in his head. And suddenly it made it, sending a shocking wave of pain through his whole body.

Helga—Christ, Helga had been with him!

He forced his eyes open and sat up abruptly, aware that he was calling out her name. Ice, chipped from one of the cakes remaining under grass straw in the springhouse, cascaded from a towel atop his head and over him to the floor.

He was on the deep, home-tanned cowhide divan in Spencer Stanton's office, a room which had once been his when the Corona house was smaller, before Helga Cagle had come out of the malpais. 'Mana and Raul Archuleta's wife sat flanking the low-trimmed lamp on the table between them. They looked weary and he thought they had been dozing.

"Helga—" he said again and put a hand to the top of his head.

Somebody had barbered him up like a scalped rabbit and a bandage was compressed there, its straps bound under his chin. Mama Archuleta had knelt and was picking up the spilled ice from the stone-flagged floor.

"Take it easy, Jaime," 'Mana Stanton said gently. "You've had a close one."

"God damn it, where's Helga?" he repeated harshly. "Is she all right?"

"She's gone, Jaime," 'Mana answered. "They took her with them, whoever they were."

"You don't know?"

"Nobody saw them. Or heard the shot that creased you. I don't think they hurt her, but they left you for dead and meant it that way."

"Would have been, too, if that bullet had been a thumbnail lower," Mama Archuleta said, demonstrating the measurement. "You could lay a whiphandle in the furrow it plowed in your scalp."

He put an exploratory hand to the bandage again and winced.

"Jesus!" he grunted. "How many?"

"Half a dozen," 'Mana said heavily. "A dozen. Nobody's sure. It was after dark when the boys found you. The tracks got pretty well scuffed up, I'm afraid."

Jaime nodded and hung his aching head in his hands, but that didn't help. He lifted it again and pointed to a crudely shaped bottle of Simeon Turley's whiskey from the Taos valley. Turley had been killed and his mill and distillery burned in the revolt which had cost Governor Bent his life. When the Corona stock of Taos Lightning was gone, there would be no more. He supposed it was a sacrilege of sorts, but he needed a drink.

"You saving that whiskey for somebody special?"

'Mana took the bottle from the shelf and poured a full thumbler. He drank it like water and shuddered. He glanced at the windows. They were already graying a little. Twelve, thirteen hours. Maybe a little more. A long time. A long start.

"Sons of bitches!" he said savagely.

"You can go back home, now, *mamasita*," 'Mana told Raul Archuleta's wife, "He's all right. It will be light soon and your little ones will be waking up."

The woman moved on soundless bare feet out into the big main room and quietly left the house. 'Mana offered the bottle again. Jaime shook his head. His wits were already addled enough and he already had sufficient for which to blame himself. Drygulched on grass he knew as well as his own reflection in a mirror. They must have been so close he should have smelled their stink. And practically in sight of the Corona house.

'Mana went out into the main room and across to the kitchen in the other wing. Jaime could hear her moving about there. Putting coffee on to boil, he thought. The tumbler of Turley's whiskey was beginning to take hold. The hammering, bone-grinding ache in his head was beginning to recede a little. But not even Taos Lightning could do anything about Helga.

He withstood his self-accusative torment for a few minutes more. Then the aromatic magnet of brewing fresh-ground coffee drew him. He snuffed the now needless lamp in the office and crossed in the thin, false-dawn light after 'Mana to the kitchen, finding to his grim self-satisfaction enroute that he was not as weak and unsteady as he feared he might be. His gun and belt were missing and he wondered about that. He would damned soon need them.

'Mana was at the work table under the kitchen window. She had already poured herself a mug of coffee and an open letter lay at her elbow. The strain of the night was deep-marked in her face and figure. In this flat, unshadowed light he could for the first time see the physical etching of the ten years difference in age which lay between them.

She was a women he had once loved. Worshipfully, as a boy does. The most beautiful woman he believed he had ever seen. And for all his gratitude and loyalty, he had for a time felt his hot young jealousy toward Spence over that.

Helga had her part in that, too, though she could scarcely know it. Now she was gone. They had thought he was dead out there, too, and had left him so. But he wasn't. Not by a damned sight.

The bastards would find that out. To the last man, by God. Sooner than they thought. Soon enough, he hoped. Soon enough, he prayed. Soon enough.

'Mana brought him a mug from the pot on the stove. He sipped and burned his mouth, but noted with further satisfaction that his grip was firm and his hand steady. 'Mana wordlessly pushed the letter at her elbow across to him. He recognized Spencer Stanton's hand and glanced quickly up at her.

"The stage, last night," she said. "Before—"

He nodded and spread the sheet, studying each line carefully, so as to miss nothing. He had barely reached Spence's signature and the full import of his message when a knock sounded on the door. 'Mana crossed and unbarred it. Raul Archuleta stood at the threshold, hat in hand. Jaime's belt and gun were looped over his shoulder. Behind him, in the yard, was a body of silent, grim-faced riders, saddlerigged for a long trail, if need be. Every able-bodied man on the Corona. Even then, some were barely old enough to sit a hard-riding seat and carry a gun. Jaime saw his own saddle on a riderless fresh horse among them, a trail-kit made up on the cantle.

"Your pardon, *patrona*," Raul said to 'Mana and then spoke past her to Jaime. "It is light enough to ride. My woman said she thought you were able and would want to go with us. We are ready."

Without knowing, Jaime's clenching hand crumpled the letter he had been reading. 'Mana leaned across and gently took it from his fingers. She spread it again before him and pointed to the last line.

"*Trust Jaime's judgment. He is our* segundo. *I hold him to that.*"

Jaime nodded woodenly.

"He wouldn't hold you to that, now, Jaime," 'Mana said softly. "Not now. Not if I could tell him what I think she means to you."

He looked at her in dull surprise. She put her hand over his clenched one.

"Some things a woman knows. Or senses, if she doesn't. I've known—I've hoped—a long time. Believe me, he wouldn't hold you."

Jaime sucked in a great draught of air and gripped his head between his hands as though to compress any wisdom remaining there.

"No," he said. "He wouldn't. Not Spence. He'd give me anything he had, except you and Tito, and then risk you both to be the first to ride with me and bring her back. That's what makes it so damned hard."

He lifted his head with effort, slowly straightened to his feet, and crossed to the door. Raul waited expectantly. Jaime reached for his belted gun. Raul surrendered it with a sudden, flooding smile of relief at a justified faith.

"I cleaned and recharged it for you to make sure," he explained eagerly. "It will shoot. So will we, *amigo.*"

Jaime drew another deep breath to support the effort.

"Take the boys back to the village, Raul," he ordered quietly. "We're not going to ride."

The man in the doorway was aghast.

"But the *señorita*—" he protested.

Jaime's words came hard and flat.

"She's like anyone else on the Corona. The ranch comes first. It has to." He indicated the riders ready in the yard. "Try to get them to understand that. No, by God, make them understand it! See there's no mistake."

Eyes sullen with outraged disbelief and disapproval, the head of the Archuleta clan reluctantly nodded.

"All right," Jaime continued. "Now, who's our best tracker?"

"Lela," Raul answered without hesitation. "My daughter-in-law. Ramón's Ute woman."

"Send them both. Put her in a Ute dress and a blanket. No fixings. His hardest-used boots and the sorriest outfit you can find for Ramón. An old smoothbore. There's a couple lying around the saddle-shed somewhere. No other weapons. *Entiende?*"

"*Entiendo,*" Raul agreed stolidly.

"Put them on the poorest horses you can find," Jaime continued. "The oldest saddles. A scruffy packburro with some beat-up household stuff and damned little of it. That way they may get by. *Pobrecitos*—a busted-ass *paisano* and his woman on the drift. Looking for a place to light, a job of work to do, a way to feed themselves, and nothing else.

"Start them where I was knocked over. Tell Lela to read her sign on the move. No stopping except to pee or camp for food or sleep, and then only at a likely place. Their lives may depend on it. So may Helga's. And the ranch.

"I want Lela to read everything she can about who they are, how many, how they're treating Helga, where they're going. Don't follow too close and don't get too deep into the mountains, if that's where their trail goes. Drifting *pobrecitos* would stay clear of high country and I want no suspicion about them. Above all, watch out for ambush and play it dumber than hell if they're caught or stopped. Tell Ramón they must be back before sunset three days from now. And for Christ's sake to be careful."

The *vaquero* again nodded solemn comprehension.

"Split up the rest of the crew in shifts. I want the boundaries patrolled as long as there's light. Two men, keeping a mile or two apart, however far they can keep track of each other, so they both won't ride into trouble at the same time. No tangle, no matter what they run across. Just high-tail back here as fast as they can to report.

"And a dusk to dawn night watch both here at the house and down at the village. Forget the stock on the range. It'll have to look to itself for now."

"*Como lo dice,*" Raul agreed, disapproval still strong.

Realizing there were no more orders, he jammed on his hat and started to turn away. Jaime could not let him go without one assurance. He was entitled to it. So were the others.

"Raul—" The man hesitated. "About the *señorita—* her time will come. I promise you all that. Her time will come."

"May the good God be kind to you," Raul murmured, and he went on toward the rest of the *vaqueros.*

Jaime turned back to the room, closed the door, and leaned his shoulder blades limply against it. 'Mana Stanton spoke quietly from the table at the window.

"You're making a terrible mistake, Jaime. For her and for yourself. I pray to God you don't have to live with it."

Heat came up in him, then. He pushed away from the door, strode to the table, and angrily slapped the flat of his hand down on the handwritten message from Santa Fe.

"Damn it, 'Mana, this isn't any love letter!" he exploded. "I don't have a choice. I'm doing what I have to; not what I want. Don't make it worse."

She looked at him with big, somber eyes, saying nothing.

"They'll work it one of two ways, whoever they are," he continued raggedly. "Maybe both at once. They'll pull back a little ways to a place that suits them and wait for us to do exactly what Raul and the crew wants—ride right into their laps. They'd have the run of the ranch, then. Or they'll head for a hideout somewhere. Hole up where nobody can get at them and get word to Spence, if it's him they're after. That's what I suspect. And he'll come fast, Believe me he will, whatever the situation is in Santa Fe."

"What makes you say that?" she asked sharply.

He knew she did not mean to betray herself, but she was a woman.

"Oh, hell, I don't mean because of Helga," he said impatiently. "I've got a hunch they think they have you. And he'll believe them. It doesn't make sense any other way. There aren't a dozen people in the territory, off the ranch, who know anything about her. That she's even here or ever has been.

"One look at her and any damned fool would know she isn't a hand's woman, *paisano* or *mestizo*, either one. So who the hell else can she be to a stranger but Spencer Stanton's young wife? That's the word they'll send him. That's what we have to bank on, the way I see it. With Spence we won't have to wait long."

He saw that 'Mana had not thought of this, as he had not, himself, at first. She considered briefly, then shook her head.

"No. I don't think so. Many people know of me, if they do not of her. Most know I am *mexicana*. She is not. But she is young and built for bed, Jaime. For some men, that's enough. For some, all they want to risk a raid. Wait and you may be too late. For the love of God, think of that. Think of her."

"Hell, what do you think I've been doing!"

"You've given the necessary orders, here," 'Mana urged, leaning across to grip his hand imploringly. "We can carry them out, Jaime. With half the crew, by going light on sleep, if we have to. So you'll have the best of them to go with you. Now."

"Maybe you could," Jaime answered bleakly. "But the risk they'll discover their mistake and come back is too high. And you don't have to answer to Spencer Stanton for his ranch and family. I do."

Jaime pulled his hand free.

"Maybe to your God, too—if there is one," he added quietly. "Right now I sure hope to hell there is!"

# CHAPTER 4

Leading her horse, they rode rapidly up the shallow draw into which she and Jaime had descended and where they had murdered him. There was bleak horror to that. Not for herself. At least not yet. Nor cause. Not until she could get some notion what their purpose was and what they intended. So far there had been no sign of malice or particular menace. In fact, except for the necessary inconvenience and discomfort of the bonds lashing her to her saddle and restricting her hands, they had been civil enough. Even respectful. And this puzzled her vaguely.

The horror was the finality of the fact that Jaime Henry was dead. Suddenly, without warning, between one breath and the next. A single shot and it was over. She shuddered at the remembrance of the look of astonishment on his face as the rush of blood welled from under the sweatband of his hat and flooded his features as he fell.

An hour before, he had been a strong, sun-warmed white body in her arms, his lips against hers and his caress upon her. Now he was dead.

She looked back occasionally, twisting against her bonds. She knew it was wasted effort. Who could know what had happened unless someone had heard the shot and come out to investigate? How long would his body lie there, undiscovered, unless his horse was found and could be backtracked? Or they had been seen by chance from the house or the adobes as they rode down from higher ground toward the place where he fell.

This last seemed most unlikely. There would have been the bustle of the stage arrival and change of relays at about that time. Probably quick suppers to serve, as well.

The Corona was big. It might be days—even until the ravens began their ominous circling—before he was found. There was no help for her there. And none for him.

Her captors held to the draw and rode toward the vanishing sun to the first lift of the foothills. Darkness began to overtake them. They slowed a little with no apparent concern over immediate pursuit. Obviously they read the chances of this as she did herself.

They turned south along the base of the mountains to where the Cimarroncito emerged from them through the slot of The Gate. Full dark lay in the canyon. They slowed to a prudent walk and stopped to free her hands, returning her reins so she could better control her horse on the more difficult going. But they kept her in their midst, escape effectively blocked behind and before.

In another mile they were forced to single file by the narrows, a stretch of perpendicular walls between which there was barely room for the rushing little river. Midway through this, a little park opened briefly. Helga knew it well. It was a favorite picnic spot for 'Mana and Tito and herself when they occasionally rode together, and Spencer Stanton boasted it contained the two best trout pools on the ranch.

They stopped on a bend between the pools at a little crescent of clean sand which was drier underfoot than grass at night. They freed her feet and all dismounted. The horses were led away and hobbled above the upper pool. They built a small fire on the sand, heated coffee, and ate from their saddlebags. Indian fare. Chunked cold roast kid and some parched corn. One brought Helga a portion. She ate mechanically.

They let her go into some brush back from the river for comfort. When she returned, two with rifles were on their way up above the horses somewhere. Others, similarly armed, were moving downstream, back into the narrows they had traversed. One brought a blanket and indicated she was to sleep beside the fire. He eased off into the shadows and took up sentry duty somewhere nearby.

There had been no direct word to her. In fact, no word of which she had been aware had been spoken in her presence. Yet she realized this stop at this time in this place had been carefully planned in advance, as the ambush had been. If by chance there was anything like immediate pursuit, they intended to deal with it here, where they had the advantage of surprise and full control of every approach.

There was as yet no single clue as to their purpose or intent. She knew instinctively that it somehow involved the Corona and thus Spencer Stanton. That much made sense. The rest did not.

She also knew she was the most dispensable and least significant individual on the Stanton ranch. There was no critical dependence upon her, no stronger ties than time and the generosity of the Stantons. There was no longer even Jaime Henry, whatever that might have become in time.

Her captors did not seem aware of this. So, for all their careful planning, they had made a mistake. They would doubtless find it out soon enough. But for now there was nothing she could do but wait with the stolid patience of those who had seldom been masters of their own fate. She shook out the blanket and rolled into it beside the fire, worming contours for comfort into the soft sand beneath her. Presently, closing her mind to thought, she slept, meeting the well-wearied demands of a healthy body.

Already freshened at the creek, Helga Cagle sat down on a log at the edge of the sand and watched her captors come up in the warm, crystal morning light to the breakfast prepared by the black man at the rekindled fire. Whatever restraint of silence had been on them the night before, they talked freely enough among themselves now, words and voices telling her as much about each as individual appearance and manner did.

She knew and understood them for what they were. But something set them apart from the usual run of their kind. There was a difference in them. Troubled, she studied them again, but could not determine what it was. Then, suddenly, she knew. The last of them was coming in.

He had a collapsed brass telescope in his belt and he came sliding and leaping with reckless abandon down the towering vertical sidewall of the canyon. Helga supposed he had climbed to some vantage up toward the rim from which he could study the open country to the east, off toward the Corona head-quarters. And he had discovered something of importance from there and was in haste. But she presently realized his spectacular descent was purely for the exuberant hell of it, for when he reached the canyon floor he came on at a normal pace.

He went past the fire to the river, a few yards from her, peeled his shirt, and sloshed the sweat of his climb from head and torso. Toweling with his shirt, he cast it carelessly aside and looked at Helga. She was startled to feel a distinct physical impact in his gaze.

He was a big man, tall, powerful, and in his way arrogantly handsome. He stretched his arms wide, flexing them in pagan relish of the warm morning sun on his bronze torso. Helga judged by the smooth skin over the rippling musculature of his hairless arms, chest, and belly that he was at least part Indian. 'Mana Stanton had told her of this particular vanity among some of them, painstakingly plucking all but the armpits and private parts of the body as well as the beard. She did not think such smoothness could be accounted for in any other way. And the pride of a chieftain was in his carriage.

She could tell little beyond this. There was no hint of what other blood might flow in his veins except that there was a dominating, thin-nosed cruelty in his aristocratic features which she had never seen among native *mexicanos* in this country, low-born or high. He sauntered toward her, a curiously repellent half-smile telling her that to him all men were mildly amusing in their insignificance.

The original impact increased as he approached. Only once before had she ever encountered such power of personality. It was the same force of command which set Spencer Stanton apart from all other men she had ever known.

She glanced toward the fire where the rest had come up to serve themselves from the black man's skillet. All motion had ceased there, all casual talk. All eyes were on the man before her. She suddenly understood what the difference she had sensed among this otherwise all too familiar riffraff was.

These men were in the grip of a leader. An inflexible grip which welded them all together. Not out of loyalty or hope of profit but out of sheer, effortless, instinctive domination which communicated its own uncanny force to each.

Her eyes lifted to the man as he halted before her.

"*Buenos días, señora,*" he said. "Did you sleep well?"

He spoke both languages with an accent but easily. The fact did not surprise her. But one Spanish word rang in her ears like a pistol shot.

*Señora!*

All things were instantly, devastatingly clear.

She knew now why they had killed Jaime without warning. Simply because he was there and they had not wanted him. They had not wanted her, either. She, too, would be dead, if they discovered who she was.

They had wanted 'Mana Stanton. They had wanted the mistress of the Corona. They had wanted Spencer Stanton's wife. And that was whom they believed they had. This accounted for their unhurried self-satisfaction.

She became acutely aware that the man above her was waiting for a response to his morning pleasantry. She nodded wordlessly, fighting for time to think.

"I am Espada," he announced. "You do not know the name. But your husband will. Shortly. Word is already on its way to him in Santa Fe. So will many others, soon."

Helga's mind raced desperately as he spoke. They would stumble onto their mistake. That was inevitable. And they would turn back to rectify it. The nature of this man told her that. He would accept no mischance. He had come for 'Mana and he would get her.

Without Jaime Henry, 'Mana had only Raul Archuleta to muster and manage the crew in defense. Hopeless enough, even if there was warning.

But he said word had already gone to Spencer Stanton. Whatever the message was, whatever these men expected of him when the message was received, Helga knew with utter surety what Stanton would do. Whatever the risks involved, he would head instantly for the Corona with all he could gather upon the way, riding horses and men to the bone to take up pursuit of his wife and her captors with a cold and vengeful fury even this violent land had never seen.

And once the *patrón* was back on his ranch, 'Mana and Tito would be safe. Her certainty of this was equally unshakable. She needed only to buy time for his return. Two days—three—however long it took the message to reach him. She looked up at the man before her, trying desperately to think as 'Mana Stanton would think, and so to speak.

"Espada," she repeated in Spanish, fearful the fluency and flavor of her river-bottom English might return unwanted and betray her. "The sword!" She snorted scornfully. "That is not a name."

"Not the sword," he corrected in English. "The Ace. The Ace of Spades. As you know, *señora*, Spanish here has many meanings. You care for breakfast?"

She recognized the challenge and met it.

"Of course," she said.

He smiled and helped her to rise.

"You're a brave woman. And wise. You make no trouble. Your husband is even luckier than I was told. We'll hope his luck and good sense will continue, won't we? For both of us. Understand?"

"Perfectly. Look to yourself, Espada—if that's what you insist on being called. You don't have much time."

"Enough. Who was the man you were riding in with last night?"

"Our foreman," Helga answered, emotion straining her voice in spite of herself. "*Segundo* on the Corona."

"The ramrod, eh?" Espada said thoughtfully, almost with sympathy. "You thought much of him, I see."

"Both of us. You'll pay for that. All of you."

"It wasn't on purpose, if that means anything. We had no way of knowing who he was. We meant to take you alone. Or with the child, if we could." He gestured toward the canyon rim above them. "I couldn't figure it out up there."

He invitingly indicated the fire. She pulled her elbow from his grip and went with him. He was hard and sure, but his courtesy was almost deferential and she breathed a little easier. Her masquerade was so far on safe ground. That told her something that she thought was important.

These men were strangers on the high grass. Strangers to New Mexico. They did not know much of 'Mana Stanton. They did not know that she was not blue-eyed. Likely they knew no more personally about Spencer Stanton himself.

She thought she might be able to buy the master of

the Corona the time he would need. Unless they encountered someone who knew the ranch too well and the mask she had assumed was torn from her.

The group of men about the fire silently stepped back as they approached, waiting for their captive and their chief to be served first. The fare was more parched corn, steamed now in the skillet with a little water and bacon drippings until it swelled and softened. The black man dipped out two tin mugs, from which it appeared they were to eat without benefit of other utensils.

An older, gray-haired, gray-eyed man who walked very lightly on feet unusually small for his bulk came up behind them for his serving. He glared at the black man as he handed him a cup and turned accusingly on the leader.

"Oh, Christ, Ace," he complained, "goddamned nigger grits again!"

The black man smiled as he dipped another cup for the next in line. It was not a pleasant expression on the ebony face, for the eyes were without humor.

"I told you before," he said softly to the gray man, "I don't like that word. If you don't learn, boy, you're going to get your head busted in."

"He means that, Sloane," Espada told the complainer with a flash of amusement. "Huggo can do it, too. I've seen him. With one bare fist. Like a maul. Lay off the bellyaching. You'll be eating prime beefsteak soon enough." He tilted his head toward Helga. "Her old man's."

The man he called Sloane looked at her insolently, eyes appraising.

"Yeah?" he growled. "Well, that ain't the only prime meat he's got that I'd like to get me a nice, juicy piece of, right about now." He ran a repulsively long, pink tongue over his thin, gray lips and waved his cup toward the rim of the canyon. "See anything from up there? They going to come after us?"

"No," Espada answered, to them all. "Got four riders out is all. Lookouts, riding in pairs. Rest bunched at the house, I'd guess. Without Stanton, they're good and scared. We got his wife and that was their *segundo* riding with her."

"Hey, good, hunh?" Sloane said approvingly. "Even better'n we figured on. No head to the snake now till the boss gets there. Wish they'd of trailed us. We could have whipsawed the hell out of them here. Like shooting fish. Could have took over his ranch right off, got his kid, too, and waited Stanton out under his own damned roof. Beat eating Huggo's nigger grits and sleeping out here with out boots on and gravel up our ass."

"Better this way," Espada told them. "Stanton may be a hard nut to crack from what I hear, even with his woman in the pot. And he's bound to be pretty gored up for a while. Best to give him a chance to simmer down and come to his senses about what he's up against. Be a hell of a lot easier to deal with then. That's the orders from the top. They make sense. We'll pull on back to the hideout and wait him out there."

He turned to a short, dark, silent man whom Helga was certain was a desert Apache or from one of the Rio Grande pueblos.

"Longo, pull the shoes off the horses and bury them," he continued. "The lady's, too. Rasp out any trim marks left on the hoofs. Our trail's going to end, right here. No tracks that can be read as ours from here on. Anybody gets careless about it, he'll answer to me and it'll smart. Rest of you get the gear and saddle up."

He took Helga by the elbow again.

"You come with me."

He led her to the foot of the canyon wall and climbed ahead of her, reaching down a hand to help her over the more difficult spots. A short climb brought them to a horizontal ledge. He moved a little distance along this to where they had a view down the slot of the narrows and out through The Gate to a small wedge of the open grass beyond.

"I thought they'd about be coming into view from here by now," he said with satisfaction.

Helga saw two riders on the distant grass, plodding unhurriedly on hang-headed horses up the Cimarroncito toward The Gate. He lengthened his glass and handed it to her.

"Know who they are?" he demanded.

She focused the glass and recognized Ramó Archuleta and his young Indian bride at once in spite of their shabby dress and gear and sorry mounts. They were moving without apparent interest more or less along the route her captors had taken into the canyon with her. She instantly knew their purpose. For an instant she was astonished at Ramón's father's daring shrewdness in sending them out like this.

It was the kind of thing of which Jaime would have thought and she realized it would have been beyond Raul. So it had to be 'Mana's doing.

Suddenly she did not feel so abandoned and utterly alone in her masquerade. Others were making what effort they could, too. Lela Archuleta had the native skill of her people at such things. At least they would know at the ranch what direction she had been taken and how many men rode with her. Perhaps the Indian girl could discover even more. Spencer Stanton would have at least these few simple facts to go on when he reached the Corona.

She collapsed his glass and handed it back to Espada with a shake of her head.

"Not who," she lied steadily. "Strangers. Never seen them before. But what they are, yes. We get a few every summer about this time."

"Well?"

"A *paisano* and his woman. Indian, I think. Hungry.

Looking for game they can shoot or snare. A calf or a goat they can poach. A handout. A few days' work."

"You usually take them on?"

She shook her head again.

"*Pobrecitos,* they call them. Little better than beggars. Too unreliable for us. And light-fingered."

"So. Why are they following us in here?"

Helga shrugged disinterestedly.

"*Quién sabe?* I doubt they are. There are many tracks on the grass. Probably got driven away from the ranch. Any kind of stranger would hardly be welcome, after last night. Likely just looking for a place to camp that suits their fancy. It's cooler in the canyons this time of year than out on the open grass."

"Camp?" Espada protested narrowly. "With the sun only this high?"

"Why not, *hombre?* If they want? They're in no hurry. They have nothing but time and no particular place to go. They are like that."

He refocused his glass for another long moment while she held her breath. Then he slammed it closed and thrust it back into his belt.

"You're not only a brave woman, *señora,*" he said shortly. "I think you also could be a dangerous one. I'll try not to forget that."

He turned back along the ledge and she followed, knees weak with relief and not at all sure she had completely succeeded in misleading him.

Rejoining the others waiting with the now saddled horses on the canyon floor, they mounted and took to the stream-bed, moving up the canyon, deeper into the mountains. Helga became almost immediately aware that Sloane had jockeyed into a position directly behind her so that she was before his eyes as they rode, and his tongue was again wetting his lips.

However, at the first opportunity, the ham-fisted black man shouldered his horse past Sloane and usurped his place. Huggo must have sensed the apprehension in her backward glance, for he smiled reassuringly.

This time the smile was wide and pleasant and the bright, dark eyes joined in.

# CHAPTER 5

It was 'Mana Stanton, in her almost ceaseless vigil from the windows of her sitting room off their bedroom on the upper floor of the big stone house, who first spotted the dust of her husband's return. She called down excitedly and old Amelio hobbled from the kitchen, where he had taken over Helga Cagle's chores as best he could, carrying the welcome word out to Jaime in the yard.

Relief flooded the Corona foreman. Nothing had gone as he expected. His outriders on lookout had discovered nothing out of the ordinary on their endless daylight circuits. There was only silence and grazing stock out on the grass, wherever they rode.

Time was running inexorably against him, against Helga. Ramón Archuleta and his young Indian wife were already almost a full day past the deadline he had set for their return. He was hourly growing more concerned for their safety, as well.

The ominous cloud of menace which hung over the Stanton ranch had darkened steadily. The tension had become almost insupportable. 'Mana, the wisest and strongest of them all, had grown haggard with sleeplessness and her own anxieties. It was little comfort to Jaime to know that she also suffered in part for him.

The hands and their women and children, those placid, contented people at the adobes whose loyalty was in fact the strength of the Corona, were sober with fears and forebodings. Even young Tito, usually so irrepressible and eager, was silent. He stayed much

of the time in his own room, instinctively keeping out
from underfoot in solemn awareness of the shadows
darkening the bright and happy world into which he
had been born.

The strain was telling upon them all. Most of all
upon Jaime Henry, who had once believed himself
tough enough to withstand any duress without a
clouding of judgment.

Jaime watched Spence Stanton ride in at the head of
a cavalcade of men, their riding relays carried with
them, as the old Spanish of the high country had always done when distance was great and speed para-
mount. Eager hands came running up from the adobes
to take over the horses as weary riders stepped stiffly
down. Worried brown faces were bright and hopeful
now. The *patrón* was home.

Jaime could not share their degree of faith. He knew
—as 'Mana Stanton surely must—that however big a
shadow he cast across this land, the master of the
Corona was but one man. The *paisanos* believed that
God walked with Spencer Stanton. Jaime knew better.
Twice—three times—in Jaime's memory Spence had
nearly died in defense of his land. His respect for
Stanton was boundless—but so was his respect for re-
ality.

He studied the men Spence had brought with him.
He had come by way of Mora. Abelardo and the *vaqueros* from the lower ranch were among the dismounting riders. All of them, he saw, leaving the
Corona open and defenseless to the south.

There was Sol Wetzel. Hair even whiter now; thin
features even more sharp; pale, quick eyes more
shrewd. Now the most successful and important trader
in Santa Fe.

There was also Heggie Duncan, a great, red giant of
a Scot who had been doing a good commission business in horse and cattle trading since the Yanke occu-
pation. A mercurial and dangerous man when aroused,
but a good friend.

Both were important men in the capitol. In the affairs of the territory as well, he supposed. Jaime could understand Stanton's moral need to have these friends with him, but he felt a deep disappointment. Almost an anger. Friends, yes; but no troopers, no officers of government, no evidence of official sanction and support to warn those who had struck against them. It was a grave omission, needlessly increasing the odds against them.

Jaime knew his boss's return freed him. Presently it would release the hot, vibrating spring wound tight to breaking point within him. In a few minutes, an hour or two at most, he would be able to shed the burden of responsibility Spence's absence had clamped upon him. The helplessness would be gone, leaving only a personal job of work to get at and the freedom to do so.

But in this moment of arrival, his first concern remained the Corona. He knew by the white set of Stanton's features as he surrendered his horse that they had, as he had suspected, sent Spence word it was 'Mana who had been taken. Helga, then, had understood the situation in which she found herself. She had been able to keep up the pretense afforded her by her captors' mistake.

At least that long. Until their messenger had been sent off. She had been able to do that much in repayment of what she owed the Stantons.

Jaime sympathized with the urgency which had driven Spence Stanton from Santa Fe. It had been driving Jaime, himself, since the moment Helga had been taken. The endless hours, the precious days during which his duty to this man and his ranch would not let him respond to the crying need within.

But he bitterly wished Spence had held himself in check as he had been forced to do. At least long enough to have used his head. Long enough to have gathered some muscle in Santa Fe. Official muscle.

He had the influence to do it, the friends, the right to demand it as his due. The Corona, his own stature, his service to the organization of the territory, his Yankee blood, and his favor with the military command would have ensured that. If he had just taken the little time it might have required. Enough muscle—a whole damned cavalry detachment, if necessary—to do it right, once and for all, so that it would never have to be done again.

But he had not. He had brought only this hastily rounded up few. And with the exception of Abelardo, they were the wrong men for what should be done. There was no way to remedy it, now. Not soon enough. So what should have been a task for many competent and vengeful men now fell to one, alone. The defense of the Corona, as always, must still come first. Jaime shrugged heavily, accepting this because this was the way it had to be.

'Mana Stanton came running from the house. Jaime saw the white strain vanish from Stanton as his wife rushed to him. He needed no explanation. The rancher's one great concern was gone with the feel of her in his arms again.

With 'Mana unharmed beside him, the Corona and all upon it would survive. That certainty was in Stanton's carriage and the lift of his head as he straightened.

Jaime envied him the moment. But it was short-lived. Jaime had no patience for words now, but he knew they had to be said and heard and considered. Plans had to be made. It was the last duty he owed here.

All else he owed to himself and to the girl who had so suddenly and inexplicably given generously a little of herself in the warm afternoon sun that agonizingly little while ago among the willows on the grassy bank of the Cimarroncito.

He followed Abelardo and the two men from Santa Fe after Spencer Stanton and his wife into the fortress of their house.

"One thing," Spencer Stanton said at length, "they won't harm her."

"As long as they still think she's your wife," Jaime corrected. "She can't keep that up too long."

"It won't take us long," the rancher said assuredly. "First thing's to figure which direction they took, where they're likely headed, and how many of them there are. The hell with who, for now. And go from there."

"I may have already taken care of that," Jaime told him quietly. "If Ramon and Lela make it back."

"Good," Stanton approved. "But we won't wait. Either way, we'll start as soon as it's light in the morning. Try to pick up Ramón and his wife, if they haven't shown up. We'll take Duncan and our whole damned outfit. From both ranches. Leave Wetzel and Abelardo here with 'Mana and Amelio and the women forted up in the house. With Abelardo handling it, they can hold off anything for a day or two."

"A day or two!" Jaime cut in harshly. "They have a full four days' start on us!"

"They may not have holed up that far away. I've a hunch they're up on the mountains, where they can keep an eye on us here."

"Hell, Spence, face it. You can't chance a hunch. Too damned easy to be wrong. You can't take the whole crew and leave the Corona unprotected. You can't hang responsibility for the ranch and 'Mana and Tito and the rest of the women and kids on Sol and Abelardo and old Amelio. That's your responsibility. Like it was mine till you showed up."

Wearied by anxiety and the punishment of his long, hard ride, Stanton's back humped like a boss-bull facing a young one invading his side of the herd.

"God damn it, Jaime, shut up and listen!" he snapped. "I'm back and you're not in the saddle anymore."

"The hell I'm not. But it's my own saddle now, thank God. You're doing it all wrong. I'd rather have

'Lardo and Heggie Duncan with me than the lot, excepting you, Spence. But you've got to have 'Lardo and Heggie's got no business being here in the first place. So I'm going it alone. Now. Soon as I can slap a kit together and get a saddle up. Before any more time is lost."

"Alone?" Stanton roared. He shook his head as though to regain control of rising irritation and impatience. "Your brains must have leaked out that hole they blew in your head. Who the devil you think you are—God Almighty? Don't pick a time like this to tell me what you or me or anybody else on this ranch is going to do or not do!"

"Look, Spence," Jaime begged wearily. "Sit tight for a minute, for Christ's sake. I've had almost four days to think this out. The hardest thinking I've ever had to do. You haven't, because you haven't even known what the situation really is until the last hour. My way's the only one left open to any of us now."

Stanton's head shook slowly and stubbornly from side to side, bull-like again.

"You obstinate fool, don't you realize I want that girl back safe and as quickly as you do? Don't talk to me about responsibility. They stole her from under my roof. Do you think for a moment that I'll let one man —even you, boy—risk harm to her and maybe even her life for his own stupid, stubborn vanity? The surest way to get her back, fast and unharmed, is to use every ounce of force at my command. We ride at first light. All of us. Together."

Jaime's weariness was an increasing burden. Words. So necessary to others. So useless. Yet he had to say them because he knew he was right.

"You'll be playing squarely into their hands, just like you have been doing, ever since they got word to you in Santa Fe."

Heggie Duncan leaned forward sharply.

"Here, now, laddie!" the great, red Scot rumbled. "This gets none of us anywhere. Do na fray a mon without reason. The message merely said, 'We have your wife. She will na be harmed, for now. You will hear from us in a few days. Be ready to trade.'—"

"Written on a card from a playing deck," Wetzel added.

"He came to his two best friends," the Scot continued. "We came with him to help him find his missus. We find now she is safe, but a lass has been taken. So we go after her, instead. I dinna ken a difference. What mistake's in that?"

"What the hell you expect, boy?" Sol Wetzel asked. "We've both known him long enough. He's Spencer Stanton."

"Exactly," Jaime agreed. "I knew you'd be here, as fast as you could make it, Spence. I think they did, too. Counted on it. Which means to me this is where they want you. Otherwise their message would have told you something else. Your letter to 'Mana said you all think another revolt is cooking up. That you thought the leaders might move against some of you, personally. Something about your political influence. Any of you. Or all."

Jaime paused and looked pleadingly at the only man for whom he'd ever worked for wages, the head of the only real family he had ever known.

"Well, *patrón*," he said, "I may be a dumb hill boy, a cow-wrangler with dung on my boots, but for my money, that's sure as hell what they've done."

"Christ Almighty, Jaime," Stanton protested testily, "I knew that the minute that stupid playing card was shoved under my door at La Fonda. So did Sol and Heggie, when I showed it to them."

"There's Army in Santa Fe, isn't there?" Jaime demanded. "Colonel Price. I don't know how many troops of cavalry. Soldiers of the U.S.A. Enough to close them in from all sides, once they've been run down. So you went to your friends. Two men, when two hundred would be more like it."

"For a damned good reason," Stanton replied. "If

you read my letter, you know the territory can't afford another revolt if it expects Congress to act on our petitions for self-government. The Army wouldn't let go for years. Whatever this is, we've got to stamp it out ourselves, before it comes to official and public notice."

"Maybe," Jaime agreed. "I don't know anything about that. Only that you were willing, there in Santa Fe, to pass up a pretty damn sure way to wipe it out, all in one stroke. To risk certainty of 'Mana's safety. Maybe Tito and the Corona, too. And now Helga."

He drew a deep breath.

"Well, Spence, whatever those bastards are planning, I think you've risked your damned government, along with everything else."

Jaime saw Heggie Duncan and Sol Wetzel exchange sharp glances. Spencer Stanton was looking at the toes of his dusty, stirrup-marked boots, thrust far out before him. For the first time, he said nothing.

"Look where you are now," Jaime continued. "The three most important men in the territory—three of the most important, anyway—out of Santa Fe indefinitely. Maybe even permanently. If that isn't playing into their hands, I don't know what the hell is."

Stanton still said nothing. Neither did Wetzel or Duncan. Jaime crowded in, trying to make his point while he could.

"I don't know what they're after. What the stakes are or how important it is. But I know what's important to me. You and 'Mana, Spence. Tito. This ranch. And Helga."

"I think we should listen, Stanton," Heggie Duncan said.

Stanton nodded.

"I am."

"Heggie and Sol belong back in Santa Fe. As fast as they can get there. To cover with the authorities, in case they move in."

"Go on, boy. You're making sense." Sol Wetzel's head was back, deep thought smoky in his eyes.

Jaime continued, the last of the words running out.

"You've pulled Abelardo, the best man we have, and the rest of the Mora crew up from the lower ranch. Your back's wide open there now. They'll have to be sent back. A blind man can see that much."

For the first time, 'Mana spoke.

"I think he's right, Spence. I've worried about that."

"You, too, *querida?*" Stanton asked accusingly. "Damn it, I'm not going to be overruled under my own roof! You should know that, even if nobody else seems to."

Jaime surged to his feet in exasperation.

"Oh, hell, nobody's trying to overrule. I know the fat chance of that with you, even better than 'Mana or anybody else does. It's just that I'm damned if I'll let you go helling off after whoever took Helga with what men we'd have left. If that'd work, I'd have been long gone with them before you ever got that message in Santa Fe. Lord knows Raul and the boys sure wanted to. The first morning."

Stanton looked at 'Mana. She nodded sober confirmation. He, too, came to his feet.

"Then I'm not the only one who's made a mistake in this, am I, Jaime?"

Jaime knew, then, that further persuasion was useless. Helga was out there and somebody had to go after her, right or wrong. Without further delay. But allegiance to a man and a spread of land did not surrender so easily.

"One last time," he said stonily. "They don't want Helga or 'Mana or me. Try to get that through your head. Just a way at you. They want you to follow, with every hand on the Corona. They'll pick the place —probably already have—and wait there. Because you're Spence Stanton and they expect you to come, just the way you intend. You'll never get within rifle-shot of Helga. And there's a big chance you'll never come back. Any of you. They'll try to make sure of that."

He crossed to the door and lifted his hat from the rack on the wall there. He faced the room again, stubbornness hard now.

"Understand, Spence. I'm not working for you anymore. Just for myself. One man may have a chance. I'm going to take it. And a twelve-hour start on you."

"*Vaya con Dios*, Jaime," 'Mana said softly.

It was the only word spoken in the room before he banged the door closed behind him.

Ten minutes later, when he emerged from the adobe he shared with Amelio at the corrals, his kit made up and with a saddlebag of grub hastily rustled from Mama Archuleta, Spencer Stanton was waiting in the dooryard. The rancher had Jaime's saddle up on his own favorite mount. The finest horse on the Stanton ranch. A deep-bottomed, light-footed mare, the first get of a great, dappled stallion which Spence had once commandeered from fighting Heggie Duncan in the days when they had been enemies.

"One thing, Jaime," the tall man said. "Get it straight. Whatever you do, you're still working for the Corona. You always will be. It's a hard thing to swallow after making a horse's ass of myself, but I've been outvoted. And you all may be right. So I say it, too. *Vaya con Dios*. We won't be following."

It was the closest thing to an outright apology Jaime had ever heard from Spence Stanton. And he thought as close a moment as they'd had in a long and close association.

Their hands gripped hard in unsaid things and he swung to the saddle. It was a little over an hour since Stanton's arrival.

# CHAPTER 6

Jaime had hoped that when the time came, he would be able to take a shortcut to some known objective, making up some of the delay caused by his wait for Spence Stanton's return. But without a report from Ramón and Lela Archuleta on what the Indian girl had been able to read from signs left behind by Helga and her abductors, he would have to start from scratch.

He rode into the lowering sun, hard and straight toward the little swale in which he and the girl had been ambushed. However, as he topped the first substantial rise to the westward, three or four miles out from the ranch, he saw Ramón and his wife moving painfully down the opposite slope. He knew at once that they had encountered difficulty of some sort, and although prudence warned him to conserve the animal against later need, he let Stanton's splendid dappled mare full out, closing distance rapidly.

The young Archuletas had one remaining horse between them. Ramón was leading the limping animal while his wife rode. She sat hunched far forward, hands braced against the bare pommeltree of her worn-out rawhide saddle as though with hurt. Their pack burro and outfit and the other horse were missing. When they saw him coming, they halted and Ramón sank wearily onto his buttocks in the grass to wait.

Jaime hammered up to them, flung down before the

mare was fully halted, and ran to Ramón.

"Are you all right?" he demanded anxiously.

"I have seen better days, *amigo*," Ramón admitted wryly. He did not attempt to regain his feet.

"What happened?"

"We disobeyed you a little, I think, Jaime," the New Mexican said. "We went into the mountains farther than we intended. But we thought there were important things to be learned there."

"Did you run into them? Did they see you—put you in this fix?"

"No. I think you did that." Ramón lifted one of his feet, stretched out before him on the grass.

For the first time Jaime saw that the old boots he had prescribed for him in Ramón's orders had practically disintegrated. They had lost their soles and the man had been walking on bloody bare feet. God only knew for how long and how far.

"These were not such good horses you had us take," Ramón continued. "And the pack burro was much trouble. A devil on four legs. Lela was leading him in a bad place while I rode ahead to find the best footing. He balked when her horse was off-balance and jerked it down. It was a bad fall. The horse broke its leg and I had to kill it."

Lela's wan face twisted in a grimace of recollection.

"With his knife," she said. "And it was not a good one."

"That is a hard thing to do with a dull blade, Jaime," Ramón said ruefully. "It is a good thing we were already on our way back down. I think the fall may have broken Lela's leg, too. She has much pain. But of course, *amigo*—" Ramón paused, his sense of humor briefly conquering his own pain and weariness. "I did not think I could kill her with such a dull blade. She is a pretty good wife, even when she hobbles."

Jaime hurried to the off side of Lela's horse in sharp concern. Her foot dangled free of the stirrup. Her shapely lower leg had been severely abraded and stone-bruised in her fall and was deeply colored and alarmingly swollen about the ankle and foot. She winced in spite of his intended gentleness as he took hold with practiced fingers. The bone seemed sound and the movement of the joint unimpaired. He looked up at her.

"A bad one," he said. "But only a sprain, I think. I can't find a break. Don't touch it down, until 'Mana can have a good look. She'll know what to do."

She nodded with a relief equal to his own and tried to smile her thanks, pale and not up to words. Jaime went quickly to his own horse, shoved his grub-packet under the lashings of his kit on the cantle, and dropped his emptied saddlebags beside Ramón, guilty in the knowledge of the misfortune and suffering the sorry animals and outfits he had insisted upon as disguise had caused them.

"Cut some liners for those boots out of that before you try to go on," he ordered. "You'll never make it on those feet if you don't."

Ramón showed his dull old knife and reached up for Jaime's, setting to work at once on the saddlebag leathers. As he worked he made his report, speaking with characteristic modesty but with satisfaction and a deep pride in his wife's tracking skill.

Yes, they had been seen. But at a distance, only, with a glass, Ramón thought. Out on the grass, before they followed the tracks of the raiders into the canyon of the Cimarroncito by way of The Gate. Afterward they seemed dismissed or ignored, without interest.

None had waited or come closer to investigate further. Lela had been free to read all she could from the marks of passage they left behind. The disguise Jaime had prescribed for them had worked well, for that purpose at least.

No, the *señorita* did not seem to have resisted or to have been harmed in any way. In the narrows of the canyon they had let her have the head of her horse. Later, the next day, as well. In close company, of course. But the tracks, which they made no apparent attempt to conceal, said she rode without difficulty. Lela thought she was all right so far.

They were fourteen, including their captive, all others men. There were no unusual ones among them. Or distinctive animals. Lela did not think that any of them had been in the area before or knew the country. Only a preplanned route through it, from which they did not and probably would not deviate except in some emergency they did not anticipate.

They had nighted at the pools above the narrows and kept a watch there. As Indians might. To ambush any immediate pursuit. When none appeared, they had resumed on up the river, riding in the stream. They had pulled off the shoes of their horses before entering the water, rounding off and roughening the trim of the hoofs to leave tracks like those of habitually unshod horses.

Higher up, when they splashed out to the canyon floor again, it was difficult to separate their tracks from those of old Indian transits. And many of these yet remained in sheltered places, so that it was difficult to always be sure. Lela believed they had done this to leave no trail from that point on. However, some of them were certainly *yanquis* or other outland strangers, for they had been careless in certain places and clear signs of recent passage remained, although it sometimes had taken much time to find them. Part of the delay in the return of his wife and himself had been because of that.

But most of them had taken great care after they had quit the stream. From this Lela thought their leader might be Indian, although of a distant tribe. Or they had some such Indian as a guide and put much confidence in his judgment. Further tracking had been hard going and had taken much patience. But they had stuck with the trail until the Cimarroncito forked at the granite base of the great peaks themselves.

Jaime interrupted sharply, realizing that Spence Stanton's hunch about the destination of the abductors might have been right, after all.

"The forks? Then they've got to be holed up in there someplace. Both branches of the Cimarroncito dead-end under timberline in granite box canyons a mountain goat couldn't climb out of."

Ramón shook his head.

"I thought so, too. But Lela told me no. That's why we followed them on into the mountains. To make sure. There is a way out of the box at the head of the north fork. Remembered by a few of the older Utes. Made by buffalo, when they ranged in here, Lela thinks. Seldom used, even in the old days. Then only by women's parties, moving camp when there was no danger and no need to hurry.

"It does not climb very high and is easy going for a small party, but three or four times as long as the main Taos trade road up the big Cimarron to Ute Park and the Moreno and down the other side. Too slow for hunters and raiders and war parties, coming either way. That is the way they went."

"You're absolutely sure?"

"They planned well, Jaime. And one of them knows the way or they had friends to direct them. So they'd run no risk of meeting anyone. No risk of being seen. That's the way they came. That's the way they're going back. Over the mountains. They've probably already crossed them by now. Lela thinks they've had enough time. Or nearly so."

Jaime was not surprised at the existence of this forgotten trail. He knew this country as well as a man could in the time he had been here, but a lifetime was not long enough for an outlander to learn all of the secrets of the Sangre de Cristos. But it was not the only seldom-used Indian pass through the granite backbone of the mountains and he saw sudden opportunity to greatly reduce the lead Helga's captors had over him.

"Where does it end? On the other side?"

"Just south of Blue Lake, the one the *Taoseños* call their Spirit Water."

Ramón finished cutting and fitting liners for his disintegrating boots from Jaime's saddle bags. He rose gingerly to his feet and returned Jaime's knife.

"Better?" Jaime asked.

The New Mexican nodded gratefully.

"*Mucho mejor,*" he agreed. "*Gracias.* We can make it home, now."

"Good. Tell the *patrón* I'm going to try to gain some time on them. All I can. I'm going over El Cumbre."

Lela Archuleta lifted her head and straightened, wincing at the effort.

"Not El Cumbre," she protested. "No one goes that way except for life or death. No one ever has. Even my own people, in the old days. It is too high, too dangerous. Even if you knew the way. I don't think a *yanqui* could make it."

"The *patrón* has. At least twice that I can think of. When he was in a hurry. If he could, I can too, if I have to. And this is life or death. It sure as hell ought to save time."

The Ute girl nodded, but with strong disapproval.

"*Cualquiere,*" she agreed. "It could be two days shorter to Taos than the trail they took. Maybe three, since they seem in no hurry. If you live."

"I don't die easy," Jaime said shortly. "Tell the *patrón* I'll have to know what's happening on this side, too, if I can. I'll get in touch with Padre Frederico on the other side, somehow. The *patrón* can try to get word to me through him, if there's something important. But tell him to use a messenger who won't talk except to the right people if he runs into trouble. *Entiende?*"

"*Sí*," Ramón said reluctantly. "*Entendemos.*"

With this assurance, Jaime swung up and let the dappled mare out. When he topped the rise marking the watershed of the Cimarroncito, he looked back. Ramón Archuleta was already a small figure on the grass, plodding painfully homeward toward the Corona, leading the limping horse which bore his lamed wife. They had done their task well. Now it was up to him.

Once it had been pointed out to him, minuscule on the soaring skyline, a man could readily thereafter pick out El Cumbre from as far as forty or fifty miles out onto the eastward grass. The pass lay in what appeared at such distance to be a shallow, vee-notched saddle between the two most dominant peaks of the massive, ragged tumble of sere crags and titanic, sharp-shouldered bastions where the Sangre de Cristos rose to the highest and most impenetrable wilderness in the territory.

It was, as the Indians called it, truly the top of the world, walling Santa Fe off from the north and the Mora ranch of the Corona from the west. Beyond—far beyond and only visible from the summit of the Divide, itself—lay the vast depression of the *Rio Grande Del Norte,* fading off into the ever-changing red-blues of the great westward desert. Somewhere on the near slopes above that huge void, straight over the highest of the peaks, was the sacred little Blue Lake near where Lela Archuleta thought his trail might end in the high, timber-fringed savannahs of the Taos Valley.

Jaime Henry knew little of the country beyond the mountains. He had himself never actually crossed the Divide onto its western slope. He only knew that it was richly colored land of hard and brilliant light and dark shadows, deep in legend. Here, among some, it was boasted and perhaps even believed that the memory of man went back to the beginnings of time. Pride and jealousies and resentments were as ancient as the memories. Prayers were still offered to strange gods in secret places and the blood of three races had stained and blended with the red earth.

In such a place as this a stranger, even in these days, was a man alone, whatever his purpose and the reason for his presence.

Crossing the Cimarroncito at the base of the mountains, half a mile downstream from where it emerged from The Gate, Jaime hit the well-marked trail to the Mora ranch. He held at a steady lope on to the south on this better going. In a few miles he found the overgrown and almost vanished fork which Spencer Stanton had once pointed out to him as the foot of the way over El Cumbre.

He took this and almost immediately had to slow the mare as the avoided and neglected track began to lift abruptly toward the great height it must reach at the summit of the Divide. Light was failing rapidly as he reached the first aspen at the lower fringe of the scrub pine and spruce reaching down from heavier growth above.

He had a restricted view from this point back over the Corona and a portion of the way he had come. A party of horsemen was riding south toward Mora. They were about half an hour behind him, he thought, and he saw that they had already passed the point where the faint trace up El Cumbre branched from the Mora road.

Recognizing them more by the way they sat their saddles than by individual characteristics, he saw they were Abelardo and the Mora *vaqueros*. For the time being, at least, the lower ranch would again be an armed outpost and first line of defense for the Corona in that direction. 'Lardo was a good man. He would see that it held.

Jaime also saw that Heggie Duncan and Sol Wetzel

were with the Mora crew. Hopefully, they were on
their way back to Santa Fe to cover for Spence and
the government they were trying to organize and push
through. He was well pleased as he set the mare on
again into the deepening shadows of the rising timber
toward the great, dark peaks beyond.

God only knew there were enough frustrating, in-
furiating, thankless go-wrong days, with the crap on
the wrong end of every stick. Nothing to earn but
wages and a short life. No other stirrup to climb,
somewhere along the way. No place to go but down.
Keeping the sharpest spade bit and tightest curb and
jerk-rein you could on your own ambitions and impatience the while. Yes, and your goddamned dreams,
too, if you were fool enough to have any by the time
you'd forked a foreman's saddle. Riding it out for another man's iron.

But there were times when it was worth the sweat
and grind and gravel. There were times when it
brought a satisfaction which could not be equaled in
any other way. A personal reward not even a man like
Spencer Stanton could earn.

The best of these times were when earnest words
were heard and heeded, however unwillingly, over
those of any others for what they were, truth and best
judgment due. When convictions were respected and
conclusions accepted without reservation because
there was friendship and previous service had been
rendered well.

However tight a bind he might face, if a man rode
saddlemate to the faith and confidence of those he
tried to serve, and there was no doubt or recrimination
behind him, he was a better man for it because he had
only to think ahead.

Like now. It made no chore too chancy. It rewelded
his loyalty hot and hard to the iron for which he rode.
It made him proud to ride *segundo*. It gave a meaning
to that old Spanish word which was of this coun-

try and this people and could not rightly be had in English.

Jaime Henry broke out his jacket and put his belt-gun in its outer pocket and buckled it up against the sharpening edge of evening chill and let the mare pick her way on up toward El Cumbre in the thickening, timbered dark.

# CHAPTER 7

They took the north branch at the forks of the Cimarroncito without hesitation. This was as far up the stream as Helga had ever been. Aware that she must continue to do for herself as best she could, she studied the now unfamiliar country carefully so as to know the way again in the unlikely event she was afforded opportunity to escape.

It was scant comfort to know she could do little else under the circumstances but it was a comfort, nevertheless, and she welcomed it for no more sane and practical reason than that it gave her something to do. It steadied her and kept her mind from dredging up the hopeless and impossible.

The north fork began to rise more rapidly and shortly pinched down to a little rill no more than a pair of yards wide. She knew by this that the ultimate headwaters must be close at hand. She looked up in awe at the massive backbone peaks now towering almost sheer above them, shutting off the western half of the sky. She was no mountaineer, but it was plain enough there could be no way for men and horses across such a barrier and she realized that their trail must also be close to an end. Shortly there would be no further place to go except straight up and her captors would have to halt.

It puzzled her that they should knowingly be retreating into such a cul-de-sac, with the little creek they followed the only way in or out. But Espada and the others showed no visible concern over the deep, narrowing course of the stream or the unscalable escarpment looming ever higher above them. She had been afraid from the beginning that they would take her over the mountains into unknown country beyond and she would lose all grasp of where they were. But now faint hope began to rise.

She knew Spencer Stanton and she knew 'Mana. Without Jaime Henry, nothing could be done at the ranch in these first hours, these first few days. Defense of themselves and the Corona demanded that. Except to send Ramón and Lela Archuleta in disguise to mark the way she had been taken. And she was certain now that this had been their purpose out there where Espada had spotted them on the grass.

But when Stanton got back it would be different. Unless the ranch itself was under threat from other sources, he would not let this raid and Jaime's death and her capture go unchallenged. It was contrary to his nature. And if he would, under press of uncertainty, 'Mana would not let him, in consideration for her.

Pursuit from the Corona was inevitable. At least for a reasonable distance. And because Ramón and his wife would have taken careful count from their tracks, Spence Stanton would know what he was up against. He would bring enough guns to retake her and avenge Jaime to the last man. Espada, seeking a remote place in which to hold the woman he believed was Stanton's wife, was holing up on the wrong side of the mountains and riding his men into a trap from which they could not escape.

With this hope came realization that even as helpless as she was, she could do more than merely maintain the masquerade which circumstances had forced upon her. Even as a captive, 'Mana Stanton would remain a woman. She would be curious and attempt to learn all she could of these men—who they were, what they wanted, and how they intended to use her husband as well as herself. Helga could do no less.

When room was afforded by the traverse of a narrow little meadow, she unobtrusively slowed her horse a little until Huggo drew alongside. Sloane, next behind, closed up at once but she ignored him. The black man's smile remained friendly, his eyes kindly, and she thought they might have small talks as they rode which could lead to something useful.

But almost immediately Espada spurred up along the file from the rear. He said nothing but caught the cheek-strap of her bridle and led her horse forward to its former position again. He rode along beside her there for several moments, studying her with narrowed eyes. She saw the distrust in them and it worried her.

"You trouble me, *señora*," he said at length. "Something about you. Maybe the way you think. I don't know—yet. But I will."

Helga shrugged.

"My thoughts are my own."

Espada smiled.

"Until you speak them. There are ways to make you do that. Don't tempt me."

"I don't intend to."

Espada's smile widened to show strong, even, white teeth. It was the anticipatory smile of a stalking wolf.

"You are not so frightened, now. Maybe that's better. Easier for all of us. I'm not sure of that, either. But I don't want you getting acquainted. We are not friends."

Helga gave him a level look.

"I'm hardly apt to make a mistake about that," she answered, using the words in 'Mana Stanton's way when she wished to be distant and disapproving. Being 'Mana Stanton to the best of her ability.

"You don't seem to mind that Huggo is black."

"Only his choice of friends."

It was Espada's turn to shrug.

"I'm trying to warn you, *señora*. Don't try to take advantage of his color. He is a good man for me, but sometimes he is a little too friendly for his own good.

If you feel a need to talk to him again, I'll put you beside Sloane. I don't think you'd care for what he'd say
to you. Sloane isn't exactly what I'd call friendly.
Especially to women. He thinks they're only good for
one thing. That's what he likes to talk about."

Still smiling, Espada kicked up and rode on to the
head of the file.

Involuntarily, Helga looked behind her. Huggo was
close enough to have overheard. Behind him Sloane's
pale gray eyes were fixed on her. Huggo nodded after
Espada and spoke quietly.

"Be careful, Missy. He means that. And if he does
what he said, there's nothing I can do about it."

Helga nodded understanding and returned her attention to her horse and the trail as the file plodded
unhurriedly on in silence. Somehow the brooding
mountains above them seemed to grow more menac-
ing.

They came to a swampy puddle of springs, flowing
from rank grass. Beyond these there was no stream.
Espada led them past this, over a hummock and
around a great granite shoulder cleft from the mother
rock of the mountains in such a way the rift could not
be seen from below. They turned abruptly into this
cleft, barely wide enough for horse and rider, its floor
littered with broken rock and treacherous going for
the horses.

This persisted for two or three hundred yards, then
opened into a small bowl watered by another spring
and thickly surrounded by dense spruce and pine. For
a moment Helga thought this was the place they were
seeking. Then she saw opposite a small bench bending
in toward the base of the cliffs and she realized it was
possible to go on at least a little further, if necessary.
However, despite the fact another hour or two of light
remained, Espada and the others dismounted here.

They stretched a reata across the entrance to the
bowl and another across the access to the bench, effec-

tively corralling the horses without need for hobbles. In
the fringe of timber, Espada kicked back the thick
blanketing of needles from a six-foot square of black
earth. Huggo went to work there with a saddle-spade,
digging a two-foot square hole to a like depth in the
dark soil. Another brought the still hard pitch knots
from a decaying deadfall and they built their fire in
the bottom of the shallow little pit.

Helga had not seen this done exactly in this way before and she was curious, but she tried to contain it.
Espada kept her under constant surveillance without
seeming to do so. Finally, he sauntered over.

"We want your husband to find us, but not too soon.
We want him to sweat a little and grow reasonable,
first. Only in good time, when we know he is coming
and we are ready for him. So we make it difficult for
any to follow very fast."

He kicked at the dirt piled beside the pit.

"Where I come from, there are no mountains. Only
a few hills. There a fire built like this can't be seen
from below. In the mornings we throw the dirt back in
and spread the needles and no sign is left."

A man named Josiah went back through the cleft to
the headwater springs, near which they had raised
some grouse in passing. He carried a stout stick four or
five feet long and he returned in about twenty minutes
with half a dozen of the fat young birds, boasting he
had killed the stupid creatures with the stick. They
spitted them on iron ramrods over the pit and when
they were done Huggo consigned the skinned feathers
and guts and trimmings to the fire and they withdrew
from the malodorous smoke to eat. It was a better
meal than parched corn.

Later, Sloane brought Helga a blanket and would
have touched her under that pretext, but she evaded
him and braved the stink of the dying fire to spread it
where there was light. No one followed, preferring the
sweeter air to be had at a distance. She watched
Sloane and was relieved to note presently that both

Espada and Huggo bedded near enough to the gray man to be aware if he stirred in the night.

When the breakfast fire had been smothered with earth and the pine needles rescattered thick and smooth over the pit and bedding ground, they took down the reatas and mounted up and rode onto the little bench against the base of the great cliffs. It shortly became a shelf which slanted across a talus slope of broken rock that had spilled down into the thick timber from above. The shelf was completely screened from below and the adjacent cliff sheer enough where no one could climb for vantage and thus spot them.

Detritus and time had filled in the interstices of the fallen rock so that the narrow way was smooth enough and the footing good. The grade was gentle and the riding easy. By midmorning they had passed around an outthrust shoulder of the frontal peaks and doubled back to the southward behind it into a narrow, suspended valley or elongated basin, still two or three thousand feet below timberline.

At the upper end of this, they turned in a northerly direction again and slanted upward across another easily traversed broken talus into a second small, hanging valley. The mountains were all around them, the normal broader views of the high country shut off on all sides. Helga was astonished that such a way existed.

It was incredible to her that the great barrier of the Sangre de Cristos, seemingly so unbrokenly solid and monolithic from the lower grass of the Corona, should be so split and riven within and she gave up all hope of remembering the way, at least well enough to describe it to others.

She noted that occasionally Espada pulled a small roll of buckskin from his shirt and consulted it briefly. After a while he seemed to become aware of her worriedly roving glance and concentration on their surroundings and amusedly dropped back beside her.

He produced the little roll of buckskin and spread it wordlessly before her on the horn of her saddle. She saw it was a kind of map, burned with remarkable artistry and detail into the supple leather with a heated knife-point. He rolled the buckskin fragment again and returned it to his shirt.

"An old Ute made it for us," he said. "When we persuaded him we needed to know such a way. One that others never used."

"Then he knows where you were going."

"He did," Espada agreed. "But he will say nothing. To anyone."

"Why? Because he is one of you, too?"

"Because he is dead, *señora*. I'm very careful about these things. As you will see. Save yourself the trouble of trying to remember where we ride. It is wasted time. You will not be coming back this way."

He pulled aside and let her pass on.


They nighted twice more within the mountains, doubling repeatedly from one rift and basin to another, threading a maze. They avoided the courses of such high rivulets and trickles as they encountered and watered at the plentiful small springs to be found in almost every depression in the upper reaches of the timber.

There was no sign of any other travel that Helga could see, past or recent. It was a high, remote, and forgotten country. They frequently spooked up resting deer, but they made no attempt to bring one down, seemingly content to make do with what Sloane had called Huggo's nigger grits.

Midway into the third afternoon, they came to a great, bald, rounding shoulder of unseamed, horizontal, growthless granite. They dismounted here and led their unshod horses across the storm-polished, treacherous footing, for a quarter of a mile making their first obligatory transit in the unsheltered open since the headwaters of the Cimarroncito.

When they remounted beyond this and rode again into timber, the trail and the slant of the country ahead was downward for the first time and Helga realized that they had passed through the backbone of the mountains and had emerged onto the western slope. The horses picked up the pace of their own accord and they rode more briskly.

Presently, through the timber, she had a distant glimpse of a little lake a few miles north of them at a slightly lower elevation. It lay in a particularly jewel-like setting, surrounded by lower mountains which were smoothly carpeted to their summits with dense, dark green forest. The lake itself was remarkable for the brilliant, crystalline sapphire blue of its waters. Almost as though in deliberate detour, the trail they followed veered away to the south around the pocket in which it lay.

A mile or so further on, traveling on a thick carpet of long undisturbed pine needles, they emerged almost soundlessly into a small, gently sloping sidehill meadow. They were well across and quite close at hand before any of them saw three Indian girls who had been kneeling, digging for roots. Helga thought the youngest was no more than twelve or so and her companions scarcely older. They rose to their feet and stood staring with curious, rounded eyes at the passing file. Espada spoke quietly.

"Josiah—Mac—Sloane—"

The three men spurred aside. For a moment the girls did not seem to understand, then they turned and fled desperately, hiking their skirts to run like frightened deer. The riders overtook them swiftly and spilled from their saddles onto them as Helga had seen Jaime spill onto the head of a steer too stubborn and wily to be brought down by a dallied rope.

All three were carried to the meadow grass. Two of the struggles there were brief. Josiah and the man named McBain were brutally efficient. Their knives flashed and it was done. Silently. Without outcry.

They swung back onto their horses and angled to rejoin the moving file.

Sloane, who had caught the youngest girl, seemed
to be having difficulty. His victim threshed in desperate frenzy. Then Helga saw that he held her securely
pinned down, deliberately prolonging the child's fran-
tic terror. A scream of protest welled up in Helga, but
she choked it back.

There had been no sound out there. There was
none, now. The others had known the utter useless-
ness, even in the brief agony of death. So did this last.
Helga quickly averted her head and crushed nails
into her palms as the gray man knelt between the kicking legs and dropped his pants.

In five minutes he caught up with them, expression
placid, manner casual, and imperturbably rode alongside the leader for a moment.

"No others around anywhere near earshot or they'd
of yelled their goddamned heads off for help," he said.
"We're clear."

Espada nodded with no sign of reproof or condem-
nation. As Sloane dropped back to his usual place in
the file, he saw Helga trembling in shocked outrage
and staring at him with sickened aversion and horror.
He grinned at her and measured with one hand an
outthrust distance of a foot or so from his fly and
winked as he passed.

# CHAPTER 8

Jaime crossed the great, stark barrier of El Cumbre between dark and dawn. He remembered Spence Stanton's account of having nighted on the frigid bare rock of the saddle, high above timberline. But Spence had been trailing two heavily laden packhorses then and had them to manage as well as his own mount. A more difficult and dangerous task, justifying waiting out the dark. And Spence had not had the compelling need for haste that he now did.

The waning moon was late into the sky, a thin, pale ellipse which gave little light in the dark black of the mountains. As long as he was in timber, sheltered from the night wind and with good footing, Jaime let the mare have its head, trusting animal instincts more than his own. With an old skill he slept fitfully in the saddle, rousing only when she slowed more than he believed necessary.

But when he emerged from timberline onto the soaring mother rock of the upper peaks, he was obliged to reverse the order and give the trail his full attention. The wind freshened and blew strong in his face, cutting through his jacket with the keen-edged cold of perpetual ice on the crevasses above. Iron-shod shoes struck fire from granite and as sure-footed as she was, the mare stumbled repeatedly on obstacles she could not see in the frequent patches of loose, broken rock fallen from the upper crags.

It was necessary to stay on short lead, carefully feeling out the way, and close to bit and headstall to pick

her up sharply when she misstepped. Even then, he
went down partially himself, several times, once painfully barking his shin above the protection of his boot-
top and scoring the heels of instinctively cushioning
hands on edged rock.

In the cold thinning air his nostrils shrank and the
chill bit into his lungs so that he was forced to open
his mouth and breathe in labored gasps. It would have
been impossible to keep to such a trail but for the frequent small rock cairns erected by earlier users of the
pass.

Even then there were long stretches of chancy uncertainty. Jaime supposed that under other circumstances and in daylight he would be utterly appalled by
the risk he was taking. But on the basis that what he
didn't know and couldn't see couldn't hurt him until it
was too damned late to do anything about it, he kept
doggedly on.

There was nothing to mark the summit when he
reached it. Only that he dully and belatedly became
aware that the way had turned downward. The dark
finally began to dissolve and form to take shape. It
was no part of dawn, as they knew it on the grass.
That was precluded by the saddle and high flanking
peaks now behind him, blocking off the eastern horizon.

It was a curiously flat and shadowless light, misleading in rough going, but as it increased, the way became clearer. When he saw some of the sheer drops
the trail skirted, Jaime was grateful that he had traversed the upper and more awesome reaches in the
blindness of the night.

At the first timber and patch of thick grass beside a
little rill, he dismounted stiffly and unsaddled to let
the mare roll and water and feed. He built a small fire
for warming coffee and opened Mama Archuleta's little grub-sack to hungrily wolf last night's supper and
this morning's breakfast as one.

In half an hour he was resaddled and on his way

again. The last of the cairns marked a faint timber track slanting off into the southwest where Santa Fe lay and he judged it to be the one Spence Stanton had followed on his first crossing.

He abandoned this to follow the little stream. It shortly spilled into a larger creek running swiftly down in a northerly direction. He turned along this, hoping its lower reaches would lead him somewhere near the place where Lela Archuleta had said the old buffalo trail from the north fork of the Cimarroncito emerged on this side of the mountains in the vicinity of a little blue lake sacred to the Indians of the Taos pueblos.

In late afternoon, low in the foothills, the creek—and a game trail which had joined it—merged with another game track at the confluence of two valleys sloping down from the higher mountains. There were scattered signs of passage along it. Recent human passage, he thought hopefully. A considerable body of riders on unshod mounts, traveling in no great haste.

There was no way for him to tie such sign as remained to Helga and her captors nor to be anywhere certain that this was the track they were supposed to be following. He had only his hope and a gambling man's sense of odds to go on. But such indications as there were brought their passage by here at least into the realm of possibility, no matter how thin the chance. And not too long ago, thanks to the time he had gained on El Cumbre.

It was a remote, seldom-used path, unquestionably originally a game trail, and coming from the right direction, as nearly as he could determine from the lie of the country. An easy, roundabout route, so that if they could afford to take it at all, they would not be in any particular hurry, secure in the belief the precautions they had taken on the other side of the mountains made them safe from any possible immediate pursuit.

He knew there was more to be read from what lay

before him. Probably a lot more. But the ability to do so was beyond him and he could afford no vain wasting of time. Grimly wishing he had the instinctive skill of Ramón's young Ute wife, he rode slowly along the new track, looking for some further, more positive confirmation of his hunch.

In scarcely half a mile, looking off through screening timber at a briefly exposed overlook, he found it. Lower down and a few miles to the north, a small lake lay in a timbered bowl. The incredible blue of its waters was purpled at the edges by the reflected light of the low, red sun. The spirit lake of the *Taoseños*, just as Lela had said.

He realized he still could not be absolutely sure, but little doubt now remained. It was enough to go on for now. He kicked the mare up and let her have her head to run free down the trail, relishing that he could at last let his tightly bottled impatience out.

He did not see the Indians at the edge of a little sidehill meadow until a hard, unyielding braided hair reata leaped from concealing pine needles to saddle height across the trail, jerked taut between two trees. It jammed his arms back, yanking the reins from his hands, to catch him under the vee of his ribs, driving the air from him and snatching him violently from the saddle. They were onto him before he hit the ground.

Six or seven wiry and hard-muscled men. There was deep anger and the weight of bitter hatred in their hands and stomping feet. Apparently mistaking his convulsive efforts to regain the air driven from him as resistance, they kicked and pummeled him unmercifully.

When he could again draw breath, they jerked him unceremoniously to his feet. He saw they were Pueblos, somewhat different in feature and build than the Mountain Utes who had been frequent visitors on the Corona in earlier years. They wore the usual coarse homespun *pantalones* of New Mexican *paisanos* but draped light cotton trade blankets over their shoulders and torsos.

One, who spoke a guttural but fluent Spanish, called himself Martagón. He seemed to be the *capitán* of the group. He held Jaime's belt-gun in his hand, hammer eared back to full cock, the muzzle menacingly level a handbreadth from their prisoner's navel.

"You ride fast after your friends," he said harshly. "Why, *yanqui* pig? You are afraid you'll miss something?"

"Friends?" Jaime protested. "I don't know what the hell you're talking about. I'm from the Corona. Spencer Stanton's place. The big *ranchero* across the mountains."

The Pueblos looked at each other, plainly disbelieving and in no mood for talk.

"The only one I know on this side is Father Frederico at the Taos mission. Take me to him. He'll vouch for me."

"This is no matter for a black robe," Martagón said shortly. "You came by the old buffalo trail?"

"No. I just hit it. Less than a mile above here. I came over El Cumbre."

There was an outburst among the Pueblos in their own tongue at this. Martagón rammed the muzzle of the pistol into Jaime's belly.

"*Cabron!*" he spat. "Now I know you lie. No *yanqui* crosses El Cumbre."

"I did. Last night."

The Pueblos consulted again. The *capitán* issued an order. A man caught up Jaime's horse and loped back up the trail.

"I'm trying to catch up with about a dozen men," Jaime continued. "On unshod horses. At least some of them are Yankee, I think. Maybe an Indian or so. I don't know. They raided the ranch, four—five days ago. Carried off a woman."

"Yours?"

Jaime paused, then nodded. This was not the time for lengthy explanations.

"They think they got the *patrón's* wife. I've got to come up with them before they find out the truth."

"*Sí*," Martagón agreed malevolently. "It is an ugly thing for a woman to find herself alone and helpless with men. If there are *yanquis* among them. What kind of fools do you think we are to believe such a story?"

"So help me, it's the God's truth."

The grim-faced *capitán* snorted scornfully.

"I don't think I know what kind of truth that is. Only that you are alone, but you boast you came after many men. Only that you say you came over El Cumbre. Only that you are a very poor liar, even for a stupid *yanqui*."

Jaime felt the surging hatred in the Pueblos. At a loss to account for it among these traditionally aloof and usually tractable people, he recognized its dangerous intensity by the soft spoken, chilling quiet of the *capitán* and his companions.

"*Sangre de Cristo*," he exploded in frustration, "listen to me! Whoever you think I am and what I may have done. I swear I haven't done anything to anybody. Hell, you're the first people I've even seen this side of the mountains. I only want to get on as fast as I can while there's a chance this trail can be followed out."

Stony stares were his only reply. The gun in Martagón's hand still centered unwaveringly at full cock on his belly.

"Damn it, I'm not lying, I tell you. I'm here on Spencer Stanton's orders. He couldn't take off with his whole crew after these bastards. That's what they wanted. Probably still do. As long as they think they have his wife as bait.

"To ambush him, capture him, kill him—who the hell knows? I don't even know who they are, yet. Or where they're headed. Ransom, maybe. To take over the ranch. The whole damned territory, for all I know. Sure I came alone. Because it's my job and the boss couldn't have stopped me anyway."

Jaime broke off. The man sent up the trail on the Corona mare was returning at a full run. He flung down and reported to Martagón. The *capitán* frowned indecisively, then reluctantly let down the hammer of the pistol and thrust it under his blanket into his waistband.

"All right," he told Jaime. "I don't know about El Cumbre. But you came from that direction. That much is true. He found your tracks. These others—a dozen men, as you said. Maybe two or three more. And some are *yanquis*. We know that is also true. But all men. There is no woman among them. Perhaps at the start. But they did not bring her this far with them."

Relief and quick hope surged in Jaime. Helga was resourceful, self-contained, and almost immune to fear. She had a good horse and few men could ride as she did. In their unhurried, roundabout transit of the mountains, hopefully on the eastern slopes, above the Cimarroncito, where the country was still familiar to her, she might have found opportunity to make a break and hole up to elude her captors. If so, it was possible she had succeeded in waiting them out and had already been making her way back to the Corona while he was blindly climbing El Cumbre.

"You sure?" he asked eagerly. "What makes you think so?"

"I'll show you," Martagón said. "*Venga.*"

The Pueblo *capitán* led the way into the little meadow. Jaime followed, the others flanking him in sullen mistrust.

Another group of Indians emerged from timber opposite, lead the horses of the entire party from concealment there. Both stony-faced groups met where the bodies of three young Indian girls lay sprawled in the thick grass.

The plain hoof-marks of spurring mounted pursuit overtook them there. The two oldest had died of a single, efficient, silencing knife-thrust. Because they had seen those who did not wish to be seen or their presence and identity known. Quickly, without a struggle.

The third, no more than a child by any decent standard of humanity, had been brutally forced before her thin throat had been slashed. Inverted toe-marks by her barefoot heels had been worried into the sod by square-cut, Texas-made boots.

"Yesterday," Martagón said tonelessly. "Sometime in the afternoon. They wandered much farther than usual. It took us a long time. We had only found them when we heard you coming."

"Jesus!" Jaime breathed.

Belly knotting, he turned away from the bodies in the grass. Martagón moved with him.

"Did you see, *yanqui?*" he asked softly. "The little one? Her hair is still in one braid instead of two. She had not even had her first blood yet. That's why I think the woman you say you look for was not with them here. If there ever was such a woman, in truth. I think she must have been already dead, herself. Or left behind in the mountains for some other reason."

The Pueblo paused to let Jaime digest this before continuing in a tone impossible to distinguish between a harsh and bitter mockery and utter conviction.

"Sometimes it is not a thing to boast about, but we are men. We know of such things. If they had a woman of their own with them of an age to be usable for such purpose, they would have used her. They wouldn't have done that over there. Not even *yanqui cabrones.*"

Jaime had no liking for the Indian's mockery or his logic, whichever it might be. And his brief flush of hope that Helga might have escaped and successfully eluded her captors died as swiftly as it had been born, his concern for her safety and well-being flooding back sickeningly redoubled.

"The dirty sons of bitches!" he spat out.

Martagón studied intently a long moment in silence.

"I still think you're lying," he said slowly. "But I am a fair man. Whether you are one of them, stayed behind a little time for some reason. Maybe the same one as here. Maybe with that woman you talk about. Now trying to catch up with these other dogs again. *Quién sabe?*"

He shrugged.

"If so, you know them. Where they came from. Where they are going. How they can be found. And we have a way to find out. Father Peyote will help us. You'll come with us."

He signaled. A man led up their horses. Martagón took the blanket from the Indian's otherwise bare bronze torso and flung it over Jaime's shoulders, making him to casual distant glance one of them. They mounted.

Others got the bodies up. A man ran across with something found on the grass beneath her when they lifted the youngest. Martagón studied it curiously, then reined close to hand it to Jaime.

"Any meaning to you?" he demanded.

It was a sweat-stained playing card, frayed and limp as though carried in a pocket for some time. The faded letters of a name were hand-printed across the pips: SLOANE.

The name meant nothing. The card did. Jaime handed it back carelessly.

"No," he lied, knowing now that he had hit upon the right tracks, wherever they might lead from here.

Martagón dropped the card back into the grass, wiping his fingers with aversion on his saddle-blanket as though the pasteboard had been covered with another's filth. He tapped the bulk of the pistol-butt beneath his shoulder-blanket.

"Understand," he warned. "It will be necessary to pass through the plaza at the pueblos so others will know we have all returned with the dead and will not suspect that we have a prisoner or what we intend to do with you. Many do not trust Father Peyote as we do and would disapprove.

"If you're the man you say you are, no harm will come to you. But if you make any trouble, any signal to attract attention, we'll know who you are and I'll blow your manhood off before another hand can touch you. It would not displease me. I promise you that."

They came at dusk to a place where the occasionally recurring tracks they followed veered from the old game trail into a thick copse of aspen at the edge of a great open plain Jaime judged to be the Taos plateau. Restlessly trampled earth, droppings, and dries of urine-puddled mud indicated the horses had been rested here for some time. But if the riders had dismounted, they had been careful where they trod. Even Martagón and his silent companions could discover no trace of human footgear.

The smell of wood smoke was in the air here and Jaime heard dogs barking in the darkening distance. He supposed they were approaching the Indian village or the old Spanish settlement he understood lay two or three miles south of it, astride the trade road which ran from Santa Fe to the extreme northern settlements further up the valley of the Rio Grande.

The Indians rose from examining the sign under the aspens and remounted.

"They stopped about this time last night," Martagón said. "To wait for full dark before showing in the open. I was afraid of this. We're sure to lose them, now. They won't have been seen."

The Pueblo *capitán* was only too right. They followed the tracks back onto the trail and resumed along it. Less than a mile out from the timber fringe, lights appeared off to the left. The trail swung toward them and began to bear signs of other recent local travel. The tracks they had been following quit the old trace here, cutting boldly across the open to avoid habitation.

In a few more minutes Jaime and his escort reached a road running off to the north and west which was nearly as deeply marked by long and frequent use as the main trace of the Santa Fe Trail, itself. The raiders' tracks turned onto this and lost themselves in the trample of the full day's traffic since they had passed. Martagón signaled a halt.

"The *camino real*," he said. "The old trade road. It goes on many miles. Two days' travel. Three. Almost to the edge of the Ute country. We can do no more here. For now."

He kicked up and they turned back from the road, heading due north, now, straight for the base of a well-shaped, heavily timbered mountain at no great distance which was thrust well out from those behind onto the open level of the plateau.

# CHAPTER 9

By habit, inclination, and stubborn Missouri nature, Jaime Henry was a hard man to impress, but he was totally unprepared for the twin pueblos of San Gerónimo de Taos. Ancient as time, they lay hard against the sheltering base of the symmetrical, wooded mountain he had seen from a distance.

They seemed to rise in the moonless dark from the earth itself and to be a part of it. Two squat, thick-walled adobe pyramids, stepped back one row of flat-roofed rooms at each level and rising four and five stories into the air. Monstrous communal fortresses, extending several hundred feet in length and each capable, he supposed, of sheltering more than a thousand occupants if need be.

The vast expanse of impregnable, blank walls was completely unrelieved by doors or windows. Access seemed to be by hatches in the roof of each tier of rooms. There were obviously no interior stairs, for slender pole ladders extended from the ground to the first level and from tier to tier above. They were the largest and oldest buildings of any description that Jaime had ever seen, dwarfing in both age and size the massive *palacio de los gobernadores* in Santa Fe and the old church there called the Parroquia.

They faced each other, north and south, across a broad plaza through which ran the natural course of a little stream from the sheltering landmark mountain. Several large, well-worn pine logs lay across the creek at various places to serve as footbridges. In the plaza, close to the bases of the facing walls, ladder-ends jutted from the ground-level hatches of several underground rooms or chambers of some sort.

In one place was the roofless remnants of a twin-towered-structure, the thick mud walls now melting away to ruin. He thought this might be the remains of Padre Frederico's mission, which had been breached by cannon fire during the revolt in which Governor Bent had been murdered.

At the entrance to the plaza new walls were going up, the ground plan indicating a new chapel to replace the old. He watched guardedly for some sign of 'Mana Stanton's old friend and confessor, but the priest was nowhere in evidence. With a strong premonition he was desperately going to need a good and influential friend here, he was sharply disappointed.

Two large bonfires lighted the plaza as Jaime rode in among Martagón and his companions, three of them riding with the bodies they had found in the grass before them across their saddles. These three turned aside. Women came from the nearest fire to meet them and took down their lifeless burdens. The horsemen reined back to rejoin the cavalcade.

There were many people of all ages and sexes about the fires. Many more were standing along the walls of the two great houses and the stepped-back tiers above, even to the highest. Motionless shadows in the flickering, fitful light. There was absolute, uncanny silence in their stolid ranks. The only sound in the plaza was the murmur of the creek and the plodding hoof falls of the returning horses.

The women bore the bodies to the foot of a ladder and carried them smoothly up it with the ease of long custom, disappearing with them through a roof hatch on the first tier. Only then, somewhere high above, at the summit of each of the great houses, a small drum began to speak.

It was an eerie sound, at first felt rather than heard. The air was pleasant with the remnant warmth of the day's heat, but Jaime suddenly shivered involuntarily.

Martagón led his party unhurriedly on through the plaza, the horses moving rhythmically, as though to the pulsebeat of the unseen drums. They continued slowly along the creekbank, as distant from the fires and their revealing light as possible. None of the silent Pueblos showed visible interest in them and Jaime doubted any were aware of the alien presence beneath his blanket.

When they reached the far end of the plaza, he risked a look back. The drums still spoke, but men had begun to carry jars of water from the creek to douse the fires. All others were ascending ladders to melt into the huge, terraced adobe piles of the main buildings. In the swiftly fading light, Jaime thought he had a glimpse of Father Frederico's stocky, stout-legged, cassock-robed figure against the broken lighter shadow of one wall of the ruined mission. But he could not be sure.

They came in the darkness to corrals at the edge of timber. They dismounted and unsaddled in continuing silence, turning Jaime's horse in with their own. The others melted away, without goodnights. Only Martagón remained.

For the first time since they had turned back from the obliterated tracks on the *camino real,* he spoke.

"Come."

Jaime followed. They went back into the timber for a quarter of a mile or more. The drums continued, their soft, pulsing insistence seemingly undiminished by distance. Presently, above their beat, Jaime heard the murmur of the creek again. Martagón stopped beside it.

"Wash yourself here," he ordered. "You go now to meet God."

Jaime heard the rustle of garments discarded and

understood that he, also, was to strip. They stepped into the cold stream, sucking air at its bite. The Pueblo scrubbed vigorously and with thorough care. Jaime did likewise. When the Indian was satisfied, they waded back to the bank, toweled with their blankets, and redressed in drum-paced silence.

Martagón led off again through second-growth lodgepole timber so dense Jaime had to catch a corner of the Pueblo's blanket in order to follow without running into a tree at every other step. In a few minutes stars appeared overhead and they emerged into a little natural clearing.

He was aware of movement here and as they approached he saw that several men were finishing the erection of a large, plains-type buffalo-hide tipi. They set the smoke-flap to draw in the faint night breeze coming down from the mountain and carried bundles of paraphernalia within and built a small fire. When all was in readiness, Martagón nudged him in signal that he was to enter.

The tipi cover was a magnificent one, the hides superbly scraped and tanned and sewn. It was beautifully decorated, inside and out, with intricately and brilliantly painted designs which had no meaning to Jaime but which he instinctively knew must have great significance to those who understood them.

The bright-burning little pitch-pine fire under the smoke-flap was for light and was carefully tended to give no more than necessary, so that the interior of the lodge was alive with ghostly, moving shadows, without source or identity.

More than a dozen men were seated in a circle about the hide walls. He saw that they were Martagón's companions. The same men who had unhorsed him with a reata on the buffalo trail and brought him here prisoner. They, too, had cleansed themselves. Some had ceremonial feather fans, made from the plumage of several kinds of birds with varied colors and markings. These moved gracefully in the air to a common rhythm, for the soft pulsation of the distant drums carried undiminished here, as well.

Jaime sensed that the former overt hostility of the Pueblos had subsided, submerged beneath something more important to them, now. They seemed unaware of him as an individual or an alien. Their focus was on some distant place, the target of their attention no longer human. Each seemed seated by ritual in an allotted place. He discovered that his was to the right of Martagón, opposite the entrance flap, which was now laced up behind them against intrusion from without.

One dropped a few twigs of cedar on the wavering flames. Fans wafted the sweet-scented smoke to and about him. Crushed sage was handed to him so that he could wash his hands and the skin of his face and throat in its pleasing pungency as others did. Each man produced his knife, brushed it with sage, and put it before him. Jaime's blade, taken from him on the trail, was found beneath another's blanket and returned to him so he could do likewise.

Near the little fire, and lit by it to central importance, was a crescent mound of clean sand, handsmoothed. Upon this sat a single, bursting, leafless vegetable bud from some plant Jaime did not know. It was not a fruit like any he had ever seen, but it was about the size and shape of the fat Missouri crab apples he remembered in his granddaddy's tangled, untended hill orchard. Cedar smoke was gently wafted across it as well, with great veneration.

Before each man were four smaller such buds or buttons from the same type of plant. A small buckskin pouch was passed around to the left. Each man took a pinch of something from it and sprinkled it ceremoniously over the buttons before him. At his turn, Jaime thought the substance might be hand-ground cornmeal, but he could not be sure.

When the pouch finished its round with Martagón

and was put away, Jaime was suddenly aware that the drums had stopped, just when he did not know, leaving a reverberating silence. It stretched out taut. Then Martagón spoke. The words were Spanish. For his benefit, Jaime thought. It was a prayer, but one no priest had ever learned or taught. And it was not addressed to icon or sky but to the curious large central button by the fire.

"Father Peyote, open the Way," Martagón intoned. "We wish to travel the Peyote Road. We wish to take this one with us. Make it the Road to Truth for him."

The insidious drums began again. Jaime realized that now they were not distant but here, within the tipi, under the blankets of some of those who sat with him, although he could not identify the drummers. Perhaps they had been here before and he had only imagined they came from the pueblo.

The thought disturbed him. He was tired and badly in need of sleep. The wound in his scalp throbbed. So did his head. And the throbbing drums were no help. Time was ticking away inexorably. And he was being forced to waste it. When Helga lay in the balance. Spence Stanton and 'Mana. The Corona. God only knew. But he was aware of soft, powerful insistence.

He watched the others and did as they did. He picked up one of the buttons before him, cleaning a little, fibrous tuft from its center and some outer covering away with his sage-scented knife. He put the button into his mouth and began to chew its crisp, almost nutlike pulp.

It had no taste that he could recognize, pleasant or otherwise. A little acridity, maybe. An alkaline sensation, like that when forced by dusty thirst to drink from one of the spongy seeps which at some seasons were the only water on the extreme eastern ranges of the Corona, out toward the *llanos estacados*. Some curious quality which permeated the lining of his mouth and so directly into his bloodstream. Not dis-

tasteful or dangerous so much as unfamiliar and therefore uncertain.

One of the Pueblos began to sing. A disembodied
voice among the blanketed figures about him. Jaime
chewed mechanically until the button in his mouth
was reduced to a fine paste. He spat this as others did
into the palm of his hand, rolled it into a little ball,
and swallowed it.

The singer finished his song and another took over
with his own. Then another, the privilege seeming to
move from man to man in order about the fire. Jaime
chewed up the other three buttons before him in the
same way. He closed his heavy-lidded eyes and
slumped wearily in his blanket. His turn at song
passed him by without a break in the rhythm of the
drums.

A curious and unwanted feeling of well-being began
to slowly well in him. The throbbing in his head eased
until it no longer came from the drums but the slow
beat of his own pulse. The meaningless quaver of the
songs became the disorder of his own thoughts and
uncertainties. He felt with placid astonishment that he
was going to sleep in spite of his surroundings. The
feeling was welcome and he groped for it, trying to
shut out all else.

But a potent force was surging through him, making
him whole again, cleansing him as had the cedar
smoke and sage and the cold, invigorating waters of
the creek. His senses were awakening as they never
had before. All at once he felt he was all places and
knew all things and he reopened his eyes. With a feeling of contentment rather than surprise, he saw that
the sloping, shadow dancing walls of the tipi were
swiftly receding, growing vast as they enlarged to en-
compass all of this high country that he knew, even to
the dark, night-shrouded summit of El Cumbre.

He felt himself gasping in that high, thin air again,
fighting the dark and the pitch of the pass. He felt the

grass of the Cimarroncito beneath his half-clad body and his hand was on Helga Cagle and he spoke to her. A bullet struck his head and he fell from his saddle. He spoke to 'Mana and to Raul Archuleta and the Corona crew, giving them orders of which they didn't approve, and to Spencer Stanton and Sol Wetzel and Heggie Duncan in defiant argument.

All of these things and places and people at the same time. He met Ramón and Lela as they limped in with bloody feet and a lamed horse and word of an untraveled trail from the north fork of the Cimarroncito over the mountains to the blue lake of the Taoseños. All crystal clear. All reassuring. Nowhere a mistake which could have been avoided. All done as best any man could, under the circumstances.

And still at the same time, through these things and around them and over them, other voices speaking, all from the same mouth. Other places in this high country which he had never seen but which he saw now because he could see the whole world.

It was all brilliantly lighted in strong, vivid, constantly changing colors. Like a sunset in reverse, marvelously and endlessly repeating itself. And intermingling with the voices, a swelling, fading, sometimes reverberating kind of music which seemed to rise from the earth in all these places and echo from the changing, pulsing, color-splashed sky. Like the drums in the pueblo plaza, sounds and harmonies felt rather than heard.

All awesome and frightening sensations, yet he had never been more unafraid. He was Jaime Henry, *segundo* of a great *ranchero*. Across all this high, red and purpling earth, there was no other like him. He carried the Corona upon his shoulders and all upon it in his arms and he walked as easily as the moving sun across the land.

His shadow stretched before him as he moved, as vast as that of the mountains themselves. And his enemies feared his coming. These things the voices said, and they bade him to believe.

"It is not here," they said. "Not this time. It is in another place."

They took him to the rim of a deep, wide cutbank wash which cut from mountains out across a plateau. On the floor below, protected by the sheer walls, were broad bottoms, watered by a good stream. Much corn had grown here at one time, but the fields were abandoned now, the last harvest never reaped.

"It is of an Indian, but it is not Indian," they said.

They showed him men. They were in no particular place. There were a dozen, perhaps a few more. They kept changing faces and it was hard to tell.

One was black.

Two were Indian. One was of the country. Apache, Navajo, Pueblo—Jaime did not know them well enough to be sure. But the stamp of the high country was upon him, somehow. The other was not. Taller, handsome, a physically powerful and dangerous man. From some far place, a distant tribe. Perhaps a man of many bloods.

The rest were Yankee. He saw but one plainly in the changing, many-colored light. Thin and hard-muscled, ageless and gray. All gray, even to hard, mocking, merciless eyes. He alone wore two holstered guns at his belt. A curious vanity in a country where one had always been enough and a second a needless and cumbersome burden, in the saddle or afoot.

"For you the Peyote Road runs north," the voices said, and he knew they all were the voice of the Father Peyote.

"Espada."

"Beware of Espada."

"The woman is with him."

There was more, but it became garbled and the vivid, shifting colors of earth and sky began to fade. Like the songs which were a part of the music which had laced through all he had seen and heard, the peyote voices now only spoke in their own tongue and then fell away with the music to nothing but a faint drumbeat within his own chest. The sun sank slowly into the night from which it had emerged.

A deep peace engulfed Jaime Henry and he slept.

# CHAPTER 10

The sun was hot on his eyelids when he awoke. A jay was scolding at him. All else was quiet. He sat up. To his surprise, he found himself alone. Every sense told him this small clearing in a thick growth of young pines was the same one to which Martagón had led him in the darkness. But his head had been resting on his saddle, last seen at the Taos corrals.

His own tarp was under him. He was covered by his own blankets. The Indian one which had cloaked his identity in the wavering firelight of his ride through the plaza of the great twin pueblo was gone. His grub-sack hung in a nearby tree, out of animal reach. The Corona mare, restricted by his own hobbles, was cropping contentedly at a little distance.

When he threw back his blankets, he discovered that not only his knife had been returned. His belt-gun lay beside him. With it were his shot-pouch, cap-box, and powder. He checked the cylinder of the weapon and found it fully charged and capped, as he always carried it.

The unreality of the night came flooding back. But there was no trace of the tall plains tipi he remembered so vividly. No sign that it had ever stood here. Or the cedar-scented little fire. Or the mounded sand altar before it, around which Martagón and his blanket-wrapped companions had sat, munching strange green buttons to drumbeat and singing unintelligible songs. No imprints of lodgepole butts. No flattened grass. No trod earth.

But for one thing, Jaime would have found it hard to believe it had not all been some kind of a crazy dream, concocted by a restless mind out of weariness, sleeplessness, and a driving impatience. Here in this warm, early morning sun, he would have been forced to conclude that he had somehow separated from the Taoseños before they had reached their pueblo, that he had found this place on his own and nighted here in solitude.

But when he reached for his boots, he found them already on his feet and realized he had slept with them on. This he never did. His one invariable concession to fastidiousness. So he had not turned in on his own. He had been put to bed by others.

Coming to his feet, he discovered something else. The curious sense of physical well-being and peace and soaring personal confidence he remembered still persisted. For the first time since he had learned that Helga Cagle had been carried away, his gut-heavy feeling of helplessness had been replaced by sure conviction that, like all other things he had faced in his life, there was only a job that had to be done. He had only to do it. As simple as that.

He found a small, spongy seep of a spring in ranker grass. The mare had been before him but the tracked mud had settled and the water was clear and sweet. He filled his pot for coffee, built a small fire, and breakfasted. Making up his gear, he saddled and threaded through the thick young timber toward the base of the Taos mountain.

The growth through which he rode intrigued him. Scattered through younger trees were larger, older trunks. Some were huge, patriarchs of great age. But there were no stumps of others of similar size. Or even of lesser and more recent cuts.

It was certain the Taoseños had been cutting here since the building of their pueblos, however many hundreds of years before even Spanish times that had been. He realized that they had cut carefully, thinning only, clearing away all debris, even down to the stumps, to leave good space for new growth among the remaining old. In this way, generation to generation, they had been able to have mature timber at hand for necessities and an unmarred perpetual forest as well.

He remembered the rotting stumps on his home Missouri hills, denuded so wantonly in his own lifetime that only useless brush would re-root. Whole valleys deliberately burned off to bare poor soil for the rain to carry away so that in a few years even the fields were gone and the impoverished axes and plows had to move on westward, repeating the process over and over again.

It struck him that this was the real conflict with the Indian, wherever he made a stand. Not the hostility of alien races or the savage, godless practices of pagan religions, whatever they might be. The Indian left no mark upon his land and its creatures that nature could not erase in season, and he was therefore by nature enemy to all who did. Such enemies he fought as savagely as he knew how. They were the only threat to the continuation of life as he had always known it.

He followed the stream's sound to the Taos creek and turned down it, coming into the open and past the corrals into the big plaza. In full daylight it was not as he remembered it by firelight, but it was fully as impressive. There had been little stock in the corrals and few saddles and straps of harness gear on the rails. There were few Indians in the plaza or on the pueblo terraces above.

He supposed there were fields nearby, probably extending for some distance, and many had gone out for the day to work them. Those who remained were going quietly about their own tasks. They paid him little attention, as though they had previously been made aware of his presence and offered a satisfactory explanation for it.

But he was aware of one pair of eyes watching his progress through the plaza. They belonged to a very thin, very old man who crouched under a plain, unpatterned gray blanket on the highest point of the north pueblo. Even at that distance Jaime could feel the feral intensity of the old man's unwavering regard, and it made him uncomfortable.

Several older men, caked with the wet adobe with which they were mortaring up a fresh course of mud bricks on the rising walls of what he had thought the night before to be a new chapel to replace the ruins of the old, saw Jaime approaching. One broke from the others and hurried eagerly toward him. He did not recognize Father Frederico beneath the mud and sweat until the priest called his name.

The padre's chunky, still powerful arms and torso were bare. His broad, thick workingman's hands were mud to the elbows. He wore a much-stained braided belt to support a simple clout. It consisted of a yard-long strip of blanketing, passed between his legs and tucked up under the belt so that the ends hung down loose a foot or so before the behind.

His feet were without sandals and his knotty, slightly bowed legs were muddied to the knees from foot-puddling adobe in the shallow mixing pit. His thinning roach of crinkly white hair was already matted with the sweat of honest labor at this early hour. Deep concern was in his eyes and relief in his voice as Jaime dismounted for a mutual *abrazo* of greeting.

"Ah, *hijo mio,*" the padre exclaimed, pounding Jaime repeatedly on the back with both hands in the midst of the muddy embrace, "I was afraid you would not pass this way again."

"Again? Then you knew I was here. You saw me come through last night."

"But of course. You are no Indian. Not to these old eyes. There are times I am quicker than a Taoseño, no matter how Martagón meant that it should look. But I dared not speak out. As usual, these days, they tell me nothing. A word might have made you trouble. *Qué pasa*, Jaime? What brings you here—in this way?"

"It's a long story, Padre, and I've only got half of it, if that much. I need help. All you can give me. In a hurry."

"The Corona?"

Jaime nodded. Father Frederico glanced quickly about. Jaime's eyes, rising, saw that the old man in the gray blanket had started slowly and carefully down the ladders of the north pueblo.

"Come," the priest said, gesturing toward the nearest of the single-log footbridges across the creek bisecting the plaza. "It is a public place and not many crossing at this hour. They let me work on the chapel, but little else, these days. If we sit there, they will not think we talk against them. That worries them. They are afraid, *amigo*."

They left the Corona mare ground-tied where she stood and crossed to the bridge, seating themselves there. High above, on the north pueblo, the old man in the gray blanket continued to make his way downward, painfully but with great dignity, from ladder to ladder and terrace to terrace.

"Tell me all," Father Frederico urged when they were seated. "Everything. From the beginning. It is very important, I think."

Omitting the details of his meeting with Helga Cagle on the banks of the Cimarroncito as hardly within the priest's understanding, Jaime swiftly and tersely sketched the girl's capture, Spencer Stanton's return to the ranch, and his own pursuit over the mountains. Because he himself understood it so little, he gave particular attention to all that had happened after Martagón and his companions had snared him from his saddle on the old game trail above the blue spirit lake of the Taoseños.

Father Frederico grasped at once the uncertainties which dictated that Spencer Stanton and the crew remain at the Corona.

"Wise," he said. "Very wise. And necessary. One would think that an end to war would bring peace. But the fighting often goes on long after the armies have moved on to other battles. It has always been so, I fear. It is nearly two thousand years since Calvary, and still we humble men of the cloth fight the forces of evil.

"The new *yanqui* flag is not enough here. Not yet. Other enemies are abroad in the land. They must be found and destroyed. 'Mana and her husband must defend the Corona before their own lives. It is the gateway to New Mexico. If it was lost to other hands, so be it the territory. And I who say it am Spanish. But it is so."

"The hell with that," Jaime said grimly. "That's for them. I'm here after Helga. That's all I give a damn about."

"You say that, of course, however profanely, my son," the priest agreed without offense. "A man and a woman. The curse of the original sin, visited upon us all. Yes. You think it, even believe it.

"But it is the Corona you are really here for. You are its *segundo*. If you must fight, it is for the Corona you will put down your life. If need must be, you would expect the Cagle girl to do the same. It is the way we are made. It is God's will."

"Not while I have anything to say about it!" Jaime snapped. "Damn it, Padre, I want help, not sky-talk. For Helga. Do you have any idea who these men might be? Any strangers in the valley? Any place they might have taken her? Anything."

"How would I learn? From my people here?" The priest shook his head sadly. "No. I've lost their confidence. The color of my skin. The language I speak. They're too frightened to return to me. They tell me nothing. But here comes one who may know if any soul in Taos does."

He inclined his head toward the plaza. Jaime turned. The old man from the rooftop was crossing to-

ward them. He walked very slowly but erect, without
assistance of a staff. A living image of the pride and
antiquity of his people.

"Understand," Father Frederico murmured swiftly.
"Few *yanquis* do. It has taken me a long time, myself.
It is thought the governor of the pueblo is the power,
here. But it is not so. Men live, marry, die, and face
punishment by this old man's word. He is the *cacique*.
The medicine man.

"It is a religious thing to them. Like me, he is their
priest. He knows all things. I do not, *amigo*. He was
born here. More than a century ago, I think. His father
and grandfathers before him. I have had only forty
years. If you are to be told, he will tell you."

Father Frederico came respectfully to his feet as the
old man approached. Jaime did likewise. The *cacique*
seated himself and signaled them to resume their
places. He spoke in a voice cracked by a lifetime of in-
cantation and ritual song.

"Who are you?" he asked Jaime.

Jaime glanced at Father Frederico, who nodded en-
couragement.

"I think you know. *Segundo* on the Stanton ranch.
The Corona. On the other side of the mountains. Following the trail of those who stole a white woman
there."

'I know nothing," the cracked old voice denied flatly. "If it is true, it is a *yanqui* matter. Go to *yanquis*.
You are not wanted here."

"The same ones killed three of your young girls who
were up after roots on the old buffalo trail. Some of
your men under one called Martagón brought the
bodies in with me last night."

"Yes. I saw your boots. They were not moccasins in
spite of the blanket. But our young girls all live. None
have been killed. You have had a dream. Where did
you sleep?"

"In a tipi. Back in the woods. A plains tipi. I drifted

off during some kind of a ceremonial Martagón and some others were holding."

"No," the old *cacique* said imperturbably. "As I said, you have had a dream. We are Taoseños. There are no tipis, here. We do not use them. We have nothing of the plains people. Our ceremonials are for *kivas*. No stranger ever witnesses them. Martagón and the foolish ones who follow him were not there. They forgot the True Road and were sent to the blue lake until they learn it again."

Jaime started to speak. The Indian held up a silencing hand.

"You were seen this morning in a small clearing. You were asleep on your own saddle, in your own blankets, your arms at hand and your horse nearby. Just as you camped. Alone."

"Now wait a damned minute—!" Jaime protested.

"You have had a recent injury to your head," the Pueblo continued calmly. "It may be that. Or the altitude. You have lately crossed El Cumbre. Many men have strange dreams in this valley. Do not wonder at that. It is a very old place. There are many spirits. Some are evil. There is much danger here if you do not follow the right road."

The old man rose to his feet, drawing his blanket about him. Jaime could hear the ancient joints of his loosely skin-wrapped skeleton creak.

"Go home to your own country. By the trade road, so that others can see that you are on your way. Take the greeting of their friend, the black-robe, here, to those who sent you. Tell them you found nothing. Tell them the woman you seek is not here."

The Pueblo walked a few feet away, halted, and turned.

"These are wise words. Heed them. Do not dream again, my friend. You may not awaken."

The *cacique* moved on away. Jaime impatiently waited him out of earshot.

"The hell those *niñas* weren't killed!" he growled. "The hell that tipi wasn't there. The lying old bastard."

"Whatever he says is, is," Father Frederico said. "Whatever he says isn't, is not. They all believe that. He does, himself, I think. He is the Truth-maker."

"Look, Padre, I'm sure of this much. They got me drunk or something on that stuff they were eating and brought in my horse and gear and put me to bed before they struck that tipi and cleared out. The rest I don't really know. Damned if I do."

The priest nodded.

"The *mescal* is like that. A drug. *Peyotl*. Long known in Mexico. The fuzzy caterpillars, the Indians call it there. Those green buttons. The dream-maker. What they call here the peyote. A pagan rite. Very old. They think it makes them see things that can't be seen and hear things that can't be heard. These misguided ones like Martagón think God speaks to them in that way."

"I've got to find him. Martagón. Pin him down. Get the truth out of him."

"I think you did last night, my son. All he dared to tell you. Just as you convinced him what you told him was true. At great risk, too. The Peyote Road is forbidden here. By the *cacique*. We are together in that, at least.

"That is why Martagón and those others were sent up to the blue lake. Their sacred place. For punishment and penance. You would not be permitted near. That's why the old man warned you."

"But there are some things I've got to know for sure. Some things have got to be explained so I can make halfway sense out of what I remember. There's got to be something to it."

"There is," the padre agreed. "If you were Indian, I think you would understand all you need to know. I think that was the purpose. If I were Indian, I could explain to you. But I am not. Still, I will do what I can. First, let me show you something."

Jaime followed the priest across to the cannon-gutted ruin of the old Taos mission. Within the slowly melting walls were already a number of graves, some marked with rude crosses. In one corner, close together, were three mounds so fresh that surface moisture had not yet evaporated from the disturbed clods and lightened their damp, dark color. Father Frederico piously crossed himself three times.

"Dug this morning before daylight," he said. "So much for the *niñas* who did not die up on the mountain."

He paused, sniffing the air.

"I think I can show you something else. I have been wondering about it since we started work this morning. Now I think I know. Smell it?"

The odor was faint but unmistakable. The acrid stink of burning leather. They picked up Jaime's horse, leading it, and Father Frederico led the way between outbuildings to a great refuse heap downwind of the pueblos. Several small fires smoldered atop it. In the smoking embers of one were some blackened scraps of painted buffalo hide. Jaime scuffed at one with the toe of his boot.

"And so much for the tipi," he said. "But why the lies? Why turn me away? If they know anything—if they even have a hunch—why not throw in with me, give me a hand, go after the bastards who killed those kids?"

"The *cacique* told you. It is a *yanqui* matter. Because *yanquis* are involved. They want no part of that. Even for revenge. They learned a bitter lesson when your army brought their cannon to put down the revolt of 1847. Many were killed in the ruins of my old mission. They were the first to be buried there.

"That is what they fear. Any involvement with *yanquis* or their government. They are afraid one *yanqui* dead at their hands, even a murderer, might bring the cannon again. They won't risk that for three child-women whose names the *cacique* has already ordered forgotten."

Jaime nodded reluctantly in admission he understood at least this much.

"You sound like Spence, Father," he said. "That's what he warned Chato and his Utes when he sent them as far north into the mountains as they could go. So they couldn't be blamed in any way for anything that happened when war was declared and the army marched on Santa Fe. Lord knows that's long past, but he still doesn't think they should come back yet. Not till we've got something besides soldiers for a government here."

"It is the same," the priest agreed. "But they can't move the pueblos as the Utes could their camps. Peace takes a long time of forgetting."

They climbed down from the refuse heap to Jaime's waiting horse. He turned the events of the last eighteen hours over methodically in his mind, trying again to sort remaining fact from fancy.

"Tell me something," he said slowly. "Would a playing card mean anything to you? Identification for anybody who carried it, maybe. A way to send a message. I don't know. A spade, I think. The ace."

The priest shrugged wryly.

"I'm hardly well acquainted with such devil's devices, *amigo*," he protested. "Only my masses—"

He broke off, a sudden thought striking him.

"Wait, now! There was a man. Some months ago. An Indian. A stranger. From what tribe I don't know. He talked to them in the pueblo. About what they wouldn't tell me. The same talk they heard in '47, I suspect, because they tied him backward on a burro and drove him from the plaza.

"I remember he called himself Espada. The word has that meaning sometimes, I think. Yes. A spade. The ace."

Jaime was amused that the good father seemed to have a little more knowledge of a gambler's playing deck than he cared to admit, but suddenly some of the words of the disembodied voices in the peyote tipi were falling into place. Excitement welled in him.

"Where did he go?"

"To Santa Fe, it was thought."

"He hasn't been seen again?"

"No."

"Listen, Padre. They told me last night the Peyote Road led north for me. And they said that name. Several times. I remember it distinctly. Where could a dozen or more strangers, some of them Yankees, hole up with a captive white woman somewhere north of here without attracting attention? Some kind of headquarters where they wouldn't be seen by Indians, *paisanos*, anybody."

The priest considered earnestly.

"Back in the mountains, of course. Far enough."

"No. Too remote. Too hard to get to."

"A place of death, then. That would be safest. Abandoned because of that. It is an Indian superstition. The ghosts stay behind. Navajo and Apache believe it, too. All the same. You saw how they wouldn't let me rebuild my old mission because people had been killed by the army cannon there. So I have to raise new walls."

"They take it that seriously?"

"They'll ride miles out of their way if they can to avoid a grave or a house death has visited, even to the poorest brush *jacal*. Now the *paisanos* do the same."

"All right. At least it's something to go on. Forget your new mission for a few days. Get to the Corona as fast as you can. I don't want Spence getting impatient and heading this way. Tell him and 'Mana—make sure she understands, too—that he's to stay put. Right where he is. Until I get back."

Father Frederico nodded understanding of the message.

"Tell them that when I do, I'll have Helga with me. And I'll know exactly what we're up against. Tell him

I think I may have found the head of the snake. Tell him everything. *Comprende?*"

Father Frederico nodded again and gestured a cross in benediction.

"*Sí, hijo mio. Vaya con Dios.*"

# CHAPTER 11

Helga did not have any idea where she was. Only that they were somewhere west of the mountains. They had stopped in the last timber on the edge of a large valley at sunset the afternoon the Indian girls had been killed. They had waited out full dark in cover there and blindfolded her, again lashing her hands before they rode on.

Soon after, she had heard distant dogs and realized they were easing past a settlement or habitation of some sort, but thereafter was silence. Only the creak of leather and the soft sounds of their moving horses. Espada had so ordered—to avoid being heard as well as seen, she supposed—and the precaution had raised hope in the near presence of others. But they had ridden steadily most of the night and the hope faded with increasing distance.

When they arrived, she had not been permitted to see the exterior of this place, even in the pre-dawn blackness. Her blindfold remained in place until he was inside and candles lighted.

"Escape is harder," Espada had told her, "even for a clever woman, if she doesn't know in which direction to go."

She thought the place had been a house. Of fair size, from what she had seen. Not too old, she thought, substantially built, in the squat adobe style of the country. But it was in ruin, walls and *vigas* heavily smoked and damaged by fire. Deliberately so, she believed. Wantonly. And not too long ago. A few seasons, at most. The acrid odor and lifeless silence of destruction yet lay heavily in the air.

No furnishings remained. Only a few heaps of indifferently raked-aside ash and charred debris and a few recent makeshifts knocked together of salvaged planks and other scorched remnants. A portion of the roof of the main room had collapsed and lay on the floor as it had fallen, a pile of broken poles and sod around which those entering had to detour.

But the windows had been crudely but efficiently boarded up against the escape of inner light and the door was tight. Temporary quarters, not intended for extended use, so their stay here would not be long. Helga thought that might account for the restlessness all were beginning to show, even the usually imperturbable Espada. They were waiting for something and lacked the patience for it. Something they were expecting daily.

They had given her a cubicle off the far end of the main room. It was completely bare. She would have had to spread the blanket she was allowed on the rubble covering the dirt floor if it had not been for a narrow mud bench which had been molded into one adobe wall.

The tiny room had only one other thing to recommend it. The thick, slabbed door into the outer room had a stoutly trunnioned bar within. She had been immediately grateful for that, and since. Stealthy hands had tried it more than once when she supposed others slept or were absent.

Huggo had quietly found her a stool-sized, unglazed clay *olla* with a piece of board for a cover for use as a chamber pot and saw it was emptied as necessary, so she had that additional measure of privacy, too. She was permitted into the main room as she wished, for at least one of them was always there, but she could go no further and never near the outer door when it was opened, so she still had no idea what lay outside.

Quarters for the others, certainly. Possibly in other rooms under the same ruined roof. Other buildings. Some sort of hiding place or shelter for their horses. She didn't know. Only that Espada would have chosen the place carefully and that it would be adequate for his needs.

Only Huggo was present, now. The others were all outside, somewhere. He was using the hot, flameless fuel of natural charcoal salvaged from the fire-gutted ruins. Helga guessed the choice was as much for the fact that such fuel was also smokeless as for its ready availability here. Thorough as he had been in everything else, Espada would want no telltale streamer rising from a chimney to unnecessarily advertise their presence.

The black man was doing better with table fare here. There were no more nigger grits. He had fresh meat. Beef and young goat from some source. Some he had cut in thin strips and hung in the back of the fireplace to crisp dry and cure in the slow heat of each rekindled fire against some future need when there was neither time nor opportunity to cook. Further proof they would shortly be moving on again. God only knew where or for what purpose.

Helga struggled against it, for her confidence in the role she was trying to play was her only defense, perhaps that of the Corona as well, but a premonition was growing in her that her masquerade could not last much longer. Like the way they had come and every word she had heard exchanged, everything she thought might be of later use, she had tried doggedly to keep an accurate account of the time elapsed since Jaime Henry had been shot from the saddle beside her.

But there had been just too damned much to watch and remember, too many moments of alarm and uncertainty, too many shocks to body and spirit, too many miles and camps and turns in the trail. She had lost count and was no longer sure exactly how many days had passed. In spite of her constant battle against it, panic was dangerously near the surface.

She desperately needed someone with whom to talk, if only to hear the steadying sound of her own voice. Even if the words had no meaning and she learned nothing from the replies they brought. But Huggo crouched unhearing before his fire, steadfastly ignoring her efforts as he had since Espada had warned her out on the trail, threatening Sloane's loathsome company, instead.

Helga dropped to her knees on the hearth beside the black man, hoping to find some way to get through to him as she had before, but a sudden commotion outside checked her before she could speak. There were hails and the sounds of arrival. In a moment, the outer door burst open. Sloane ducked in, banging it hastily shut behind him.

She had barely time to scramble to her feet before he was to her, one encircling arm seizing her, forcing her urgently toward her cubicle.

"Into your cage," he said. "Quick and quiet. Ace's orders. Stay there till he gives you leave. We got company."

Helga stiffened in revulsion and instinctive resistance. The hand of the encircling arm hooked impatiently upward and clamped cruelly on her near breast.

"Damn it, move!"

Huggo rose swiftly beside them as she cried out involuntarily. An unworked length of rusty bar-iron he used as a poker was in his hand. He rammed its end up under Sloane's chin, smudging a soot mark there.

"Mind your manners, boy," he hissed softly.

Sloane's grasping arm fell away. He stepped back. Huggo and the prodding, restraining bar of iron followed him.

"Do as he says," Huggo told Helga without turning his head. "Now!"

She slipped quickly into the cubicle. But because

she had to know what was coming, she left the door as much ajar as she dared and peered uneasily out through the narrow aperture. Almost at once, the outer door reopened. Ignoring the fury in Sloane's pale gray eyes and the belted guns he wore, Huggo lowered his iron bar and tossed it back into the ashes beside the glowing charcoal on the hearth, smiling at the man as though on the best of terms as three strangers filed wearily in.

A Yankee and two *mexicanos*. Little different, Helga saw with sharp disappointment, than those who had seized her on the Corona. All were armed, but Espada was close behind them, his own weapon drawn and covering. It was apparently only a precaution. There was no evidence of hostility in his manner or that of the new arrivals. Only a mutual wariness.

Espada kicked the door shut behind him, shutting out any of the rest of his men who might have been of a mind to follow. He came around to face the three, still holding his gun on them.

"Just to be sure," he said.

He flicked a playing card from his shirt pocket with his free hand and briefly showed its face to the strangers. Helga saw only that the pips were black. Each of the three produced a similar card. Espada nodded, reading a name from the face of each.

"Garcia, Romero, Bailey. All right."

He put his gun away and glanced at Huggo and Sloane. Huggo produced a card. Sloane fumbled at his pocket, frowned, and his hand came away empty. He looked apologetically at Espada.

"Where is it?" Espada snapped.

"How the hell do I know?" Sloane answered irritably. "Don't ride me, Ace. I just missed it. Damned fool piece of business, anyway. You hired me. You know who I am."

"Huggo and Sloane," Espada said to the newcomers. "Two more of my men. I am Espada."

"So I figured," the man named Bailey said. "The Comanche."

"Don't make a mistake there, my friend," Espada warned quietly. "More than a Comanche. Much more."

"Whatever you say," Bailey said placatingly. "No offense. You got Stanton's wife here?"

Espada nodded.

"Nobody followed?"

"Their foreman was with her. We had to kill him. We made it difficult—impossible, I think—for her husband or anyone else who might try."

Bailey whistled approval.

"Too bad you couldn't have got their kid, too. We'd really have Stanton jumping through the hoops, then."

"The woman is enough."

"Sure way to get him out of Santa Fe in a hurry, anyway," Bailey conceded. "And his two most troublesome friends. Heggie Duncan and the Jew named Wetzel. Trouble is, those two showed back up, just as we were pulling out. That worried our people some. You sure Stanton'll come here when you send him word—without the whole damned country at his back?"

"As fast as he can make it. Alone, if we tell him to. You'll see why, directly. We've only been waiting for orders."

"They're simple enough. Get Stanton here. Alone, if you're so sure you can. Makes our work a hell of a lot easier. Garcia and Romero and I'll take care of the rest of it. That's what they sent us up here for."

Helga saw Espada's eyes narrow suspiciously.

"My deal still stands?"

"Stands? Hell, it's cinched now, man. Santa Fe's decided Stanton's too dangerous to risk dickering with. Too big a chance some leak might blow the whole thing up before they can legally get their own people in.

"They just want him out of the way so he can't get to anybody and nobody can get to him. He's got to disappear. Permanently. That's our chore. The fewer know when and where and how, the better."

"The woman?"

"Both, when we've got him in our hands, too. All you'll have to clean up is who's on the ranch. You'd have to do that, anyhow. Garcia and Romero say the crew's all old-time *paisano*. You know the kind. Grab the kid and throw one good scare into them and they'll buckle, right now. Easy pickings, for what you'll be getting. If you can hold it and make it stick."

"I can. If I have what I was promised."

"Too damned much, to my way of thinking," Bailey said. "But Santa Fe thinks getting rid of Stanton and his influence is worth it."

He extended his hand to Garcia. The *mexicano* reached carefully into his shirt and brought out a roll of yellowed papers. Bailey passed it on to Espada.

"Every entry referring to the Corona Grant in the Spanish and Mexican land records at the Governor's Palace. Even the will that passed the Mora section to Stanton's kid. Cut out of the books without a trace.

"As far as official records go, neither Stanton nor his wife or their kid ever had valid title to an acre of their ranch. So it's open to claim under good old Yankee law. What's word of mouth when you know there'll be a government that won't question you?"

"How many know?"

"The bosses, naturally. You're safe, there. They'll never be able to say anything without turning the whole thing out to daylight. Romero—he tickled titties with the girl in charge of the record rooms while Garcia did the cutting. Me. And now you."

"All right," Espada said, and he turned to Sloane. "Bring the *señora* out."

This was the moment Helga had constantly dreaded since she had first realized the mistake in identity Espada and his men had made. Trying one more desperate time to be Romana Stanton, she drew herself up, pulled the door of her little cell open, and stepped as regally as she could into the outer room.

She saw at once that she was to be betrayed by the men from Santa Fe. Her masquerade was at an end. The three stared at her in shocked incredulity as she approached. Bailey shot one quick glance at his companions. Both shook their heads in wordless denial.

"God Almighty!" he groaned.

He took one more encompassing look at Helga and wheeled savagely on Espada, a deep flush of anger beginning to suffuse his suddenly paled features.

"You stupid, red-assed idiot!" he raged. "God help you in Santa Fe. You've dumped the whole thing. No wonder nobody followed you! We'll never get our hands on Stanton. Now he's been warned."

Espada blinked expressionlessly at the man.

"Whatever she made you believe," Bailey continued furiously, "this yellow-haired, blue-eyed bitch isn't his wife. I told them they were crazy to trade away the biggest pot in the game to a goddamned, thick-headed nigger Indian!"

Espada's eyes leaped to Helga, striking sudden physical terror into her. The yellowed roll of old parchment and paper dropped unnoticed from his hands to the floor. He batted the seething Bailey aside without regard for his fury and faced her. Using both hands, flat and hard, swinging full-armed and so swiftly that the rocking blows seemed to run together, he slapped her viciously back and forth until the room reeled and she spilled, hurt and stunned, full length on the littered floor.

Shaking her head in a vain attempt to clear it, expecting more punishment and instinctively trying to fend it off, she dazedly half raised there. But Espada had already turned his back on her. A single stride took him to Bailey.

"No man uses such words with Espada!" she heard him hiss.

She did not see the knife in his hand until he struck

and Bailey fell back, wide-eyed, with the hilt of the weapon jutting from between his shattered teeth, blood gouting out over it from the blade driven upward through the roof of his mouth into his brain.

Aghast at the suddenness of the attack, the two *mexicanos* from Santa Fe pawed reflexively for the guns in their belts, stumbling back for space. From behind, at less than a yard's distance, Sloane's guns were into his hands, incredibly swiftly and effortlessly. He fired each once into the spines backing unknowingly toward him. Practically blown in two at such close range, the *mexicanos* slumped like burst grain bags.

Sloane calmly and unhurriedly dropped his guns back into their holsters.

"Kind of careless there for a minute, Ace," he said mildly, but there was no mistaking his relish.

Helga's supporting arms collapsed. She slumped forward, her battered face grinding into the filth of the floor, retching on sobs and vomit.

# CHAPTER 12

Espada made a sign. Huggo crossed and opened the outer door. The rest of Espada's men, knotted tensely and uncertainly outside by the gunsounds within, filed into the room with wary curiosity. Espada indicated the bodies of the emissaries from Santa Fe.

"Into the well," he said dispassionately. "Pack the gear and saddle up. We're finished here."

"What the hell happened, Ace?" the older man called Josiah gasped.

Espada ignored Helga where she lay in her own fouling, too sick and frightened and hurt to move.

"The woman lied. She's the wrong one."

"Oh, Christ!" a man swore. Helga thought it was McBain.

She flinched as she saw Sloane prod Bailey's body with a square-toed boot, shifting it so that the head rolled a little and the face with the knife hilt jutting from the mouth was turned up for all to see.

"Easy, Mac," he said, obviously still hugely enjoying himself. "This one gave Ace some lip. It don't hardly pay."

"So he asked for it, he got it," McBain said with a shrug. He turned to the others. "You heard the boss. Some of you give me a hand. And somebody fetch up the horses."

Men stepped forward, helping McBain lift the bodies, head and foot. Others followed them back out into the yard. Only Josiah and Longo, the Rio Grande Indian, remained with Sloane and Huggo, facing Espada.

"Looks like we sort of ran out of luck, don't it?" Sloane said wryly. "That Bailey was right about one thing. We've sure busted our asses with Santa Fe."

Espada, still ignoring Helga as though she no longer existed, retrieved the roll of parchment and paper from the floor, kicked a crude bench around, and sat down with his back to her. The other men squatted on their hunkers about him. Even Huggo paid no attention when she cautiously shifted a little to be free of the mess beneath her.

The effort was costly. Her gorge rose again in nausea. She forced it down with sheer will. Her head hammered and ached abominably. Her rapidly swelling face sent pulsing waves of pain through her. The room wavered and swam fitfully. She fought desperately to retain sight, hearing, and consciousness itself.

"I didn't get into this for Santa Fe," Espada said quietly after a moment, answering Sloane.

His usual imperturbability had completely returned, as though there had been no fury and violence here.

"I don't give a damn who runs this territory. I never did. Only who owns it. A piece, anyway. Big enough to suit me."

He unrolled the stolen documents, leafing idly through them in satisfaction.

"Add Rancho Mora to Stanton's Corona Grant and it'll do just fine. Now I've seen a stretch of it." He waved the documents. "These cinch it. Better this way."

The others looked uncertainly at each other.

"Lot of land, Ace," Josiah said carefully, his brow wrinkling with concern. "He's supposed to have a fair crew and a lot of friends. Means a lot of enemies. And you'll be on your own, now."

Espada shrugged.

"*Como siempre.* Always have been. Except for my mother. Black enough to have been Huggo's sister. Brown enough to have been a Mexican general's doxy. The rest Comanche."

Espada's voice softened.

"A hell of a woman. She taught me to know what I want and how to get it. Believe you me, she taught me good."

Opening his shirt, Espada slid the carefully folded packet of documents within, where it lay flat against his ribs with the buckskin Ute map instead of bulking awkwardly as the roll would have done. "Land. A lot of it. That's why I joined them in Santa Fe when I found out they were out to get Spencer Stanton and that he had the biggest ranch in New Mexico Territory."

"All right, Ace," Sloane said. "Reckon one man's reason's as good as another's. But we ain't got Stanton and it'd take an army to get to him, now."

"I can put you and any four you choose right into Stanton's house. Right at his own table with him and his family, if you want. No suspicion nor a shot fired till you're ready. With the rest of us in earshot to back you up and hold off his crew till he's taken care of."

Listening, trying to stifle her own breathing, Helga knew what the man's plan was before he revealed it.

"Remember what they told us in Santa Fe? The Missouri stage. It stops both ways at the Stanton place. The Mora ranch, too. They feed any that are hungry while the relay's being changed. In the main house.

"They know by now we went over the mountains. But they don't know any of us by sight. Me they might suspect. Longo and Huggo. Indians and blacks don't ride stages. But they won't suspect any threat from the east. The rest of you can fill that stage to the roof and no one be the wiser till you're inside and it's all over. Stanton won't have a chance."

Helga bit her puffed lip and flinched at the fresh hurt, cringing at her own helplessness. She knew only too well what Espada said was true. She had set too many meals for stage-riding strangers in the Corona dining room to doubt it could be managed in just such a way. Spence and 'Mana and any with them made victims of their own hospitality.

The outer door opened. McBain thrust his head in.

"Ready when you boys are, Ace," he announced.

He withdrew and the door reclosed. Sloane rose to his small feet, stretching the cramp of his squat from his legs and grinning.

"Son of a bitch!" he said admiringly. "Beautiful, Ace. And then ride the same stage right on down to the Mora ranch and do the same to whoever Stanton's got down there. Slick. Slick as a whistle."

"See now why I don't give a damn about them in Santa Fe? Better, far as I'm concerned. Only our own irons in the fire and free to do it our own way. For our own benefit."

Josiah and the others also came to their feet. For the first time since he had driven Sloane back from her with his poker, Huggo looked directly across the room to where Helga huddled, wide-eyed, almost as she had fallen. She searched the glance desperately but saw no hope in the black man's wooden features. He picked a piece of tarp and knelt on the hearth and began to wrap the meat strips curing back of the fire into it.

Josiah took off his hat and ran uncertain fingers through his thinning hair.

"Maybe," he said. "If you're that sure. But I don't like changing a knowed horse for a bangtail that ain't been rode yet. We get our cut, same as before?"

Espada eyed him mockingly.

"You don't trust me, Josh?"

"Might if I could put a finger on one damned reason why I should. What about the shares?"

"Only one change. Any of you spooks yellow or is fool enough to get himself killed, his cut goes to the rest, even-Steven."

Josiah replaced his hat.

"Seems fair," he agreed reluctantly.

Longo turned stone-cold eyes on Helga.

"What about her?"

Espada shrugged.

"You've got a knife."

"Hold on there, Ace," Sloane protested. "Seems like I done you a recent favor. Don't waste that on no Indian. I want that pleasure, myself. In private."

Espada glanced at Longo. The Indian spat for an answer and went outside. Espada shrugged again.

"Don't leave her alive."

"Do I ever?" Sloane asked, grin widening.

"By God, I've known some rotten bastards," Josiah growled. "But you take it, hands down."

"You never had one when she's dying, Josh? Right when she's doing it? There's nothing like it, man."

Josiah growled something unintelligible and followed Longo outside.

"Don't make a day of it," Espada warned. "The Ute map shows we can go right on up this arroyo and hit the trade road east just short of the pass above Taos. The cutbanks ought to keep us pretty well out of sight till we hit timber. See you catch up before we're into the mountains. We'll want to move fast from there on so news can't get ahead of us if we are seen."

"Don't worry. What I'm going to do ain't going to take all that long."

Espada went out the door after the others. Huggo was last with his tarp-wrapped trail meat. He did not look back, nor did he trouble to close the door.

Sloane sat down on the bench Espada had used and calmly waited for the sounds of departure to subside in the yard. Helga felt his eyes on her but kept her own averted, hoping with illogical desperation that pretending unconsciousness might give her a little more time to at least gather strength and courage.

The man seemed in no hurry. Minutes passed silently. She supposed there was some further twisted relish in that. She knew it was equally illogical, but every moment which delayed the sickening finality of the inevitable was desperately welcome.

She had no idea how long it had actually been when

she finally heard him move. He came across the room and passed through her field of vision into her cubicle. He came back with the bar to the door and tossed it onto the embers in the fireplace. He unstrapped the heavy, clumsy bulk of his guns and dropped their belts onto the bench. But he kept his knife. When he moved again, she knew the time had come.

She barely managed to struggle unsteadily to her knees before he was to her, lips parted and eyes ablaze with the same wicked relish she had seen when he had fired his guns into the backs of the two *mexicanos* from Santa Fe. He twisted one hand into her hair and dragged her to her feet. The room began to rock again and she half fell against him. He straightened her roughly and his eyes swept over her.

Suddenly seizing her dress at one shoulder with his free hand, he jerked half of its bodice from her in one ripping tug, exposing the breast he had so brutally bruised.

"You're a mess," he said, almost impersonally. "Here. Get in there and swab yourself off."

He freed her hair and slapped the rag he had ripped from her dress into her hand and sent her reeling toward the cubicle. Burying her face in the rag of material, she somehow found the door and stumbled through until she struck the far wall. She slid to the floor, automatically wiping at her fouled face and throat.

Sloane waited briefly, but it was only moments before his small, usually light-stepping boots crunched heavily toward her. Helga dropped the rag and clenched both hands full of the dirt and debris in which she knelt. Tensing, summoning all of her strength and what reason remained, she lurched to her feet, wheeled, and flung both handfuls into his face as he came through the doorway with his knife already in hand.

Startled, momentarily blinded, the man staggered back, his knife dropping to the floor as he instinctively jerked both hands up to knuckle his eyes. Sight partially cleared, his hands dropped.

"You big-titted little bitch!" he breathed savagely.

It was the last voluntary sound he made, for as he lunged at her again, a thick, powerful figure overtook him from behind. Two great, corded black hands clamped about his throat, encircling it in an inexorable ring of living steel. Helga saw Huggo's face over Sloane's frenzied, helplessly twisting, threshing shoulders. The black man's eyes were alight with some unholy, primordial joy of his own. Helga sank back to her knees in a sagging flood of relief.

Sloane's body fought desperately, but he could not break the grip about his throat nor get at the man behind him. His purpling features grimaced horribly as the pressure increased, Huggo's forearms bulging ever larger with the effort.

Helga thought the strangling man's eyes and tongue would be forced from his head. But Huggo was too impatient. Suddenly releasing the grip of one clamping hand, he raised it like a maul and brought the heel of the balled fist down with enormous force at the base of Sloane's neck where it joined his spine. Helga distinctly heard the snap of bone.

Sloane instantly went limp, supported only by the other black hand still gripping his throat. A great quiver shook his flaccid body, running swiftly out to only small twitchings at the nerve ends. Huggo turned the body and thrust it back against the doorframe, pinning it there with one hand while he swiftly undid the buttons and stripped the shirt from it. He let it fall, then kicked a sprawling, loose-jointed leg aside, and bent swiftly to Helga with the shirt.

"Put it on, Missy," he said urgently. "Quick. We don't have much time."

Shuddering with aversion, she thrust her arms into the sleeves and let him draw it on over her ruined dress. He pulled her to her feet. Leaning on him, she made two or three steps into the outer room before her knees buckled. Sobbing, ashamed, hating the weakness, she tried to pull herself back up. The black man swept her effortlessly up into his arms and ran to the outer door.

# CHAPTER 13

Jaime hid, dismounted at the head of the Corona mare, in a copse of upslope brush, waiting for the three horsemen who had appeared behind him on the *camino real* to approach. They were dusted and slack-seated with long travel, but they rode briskly enough to be on important business. Instinct suggested it could be connected with his own search.

They were a Yankee and two *mexicanos,* judging by the way they rode. Certainly none were *Taoseños* and he doubted they were locals from any other nearby place. They rode with the relaxed inattention of far travelers who knew precisely where they were going.

He thought he had reined from the trail soon enough to have escaped their notice. Still, he could not be sure. He was tense and wary, keeping the mare silent, until they passed below his place of concealment without a glance in his direction.

He stayed motionless, allowing them to build a prudent lead, before remounting and resuming, himself. He did not return to the trail but worked along a parallel route a few hundred yards upslope, taking every advantage he could of intervening terrain and cover which was not as plentiful as he would have liked. He was acutely aware there was some chance that one of them might glance behind and spot him as he had them, but he did not think the risk was too great.

It was a curious characteristic of mounted men following a well-marked or familiar track that their angle of vision seemed to automatically narrow. The line of a trail seemed to draw their eyes, whether directed ahead or behind, and focus their attention on its own narrow corridor so that they were apt to become aware of only very unusual movement or sound beyond that restricted periphery.

On a side-hill slope, such as the old Spanish trade road to more northerly settlements was now traversing, this effect was magnified. Like a sort of visual gravitation. If attention did stray from the corridor of travel it most always drifted toward lower country. Seldom was it attracted upward.

Jaime had often noted that animals had this tendency as well. Particularly in the wild. Unless betrayed by some general cause for wariness or alarm, it was usually far easier to trail or stalk unsuspecting game from above than to work from below.

He was thus able to match their pace without discovery. In half an hour a fairly wide, sharply-cut arroyo came twisting down from the north side of the Taos mountain, cutting an erratic course off to the west toward the deeply slashed canyon of the Rio Grande. In the distance, perhaps three or four miles away, he could make out the blocklike adobes of a small Spanish settlement of some kind. The trade trail bent obediently down the arroyo bank toward it.

Reaching the near bank of the arroyo, the men ahead quit the trail and turned upstream. Jaime turned with them, maintaining his parallel course and higher position. The change in direction was welcome. As with most north slopes at sufficient elevation in this arid country, timber grew heavier and further down the hillsides. In a few minutes he was moving in the comfortable shade of constant and adequate cover.

At this point the men below reached a break in the arroyo rim. They turned into it, shortly disappearing as they started a descent to the floor. Jaime spurred up and slanted down to follow.

He emerged from the timber fringe of brush a few hundred yards from the break and rode to it, dismounting just short of the lip itself. He found himself looking down onto the floor of the arroyo at a scene of sudden, startling familiarity. The watercourse made a sweeping turn, then widened, affording a substantial fertile shelf on each side of the stream meandering through it. This bottom land had been intensively cultivated and planted to corn at one time. But it was obviously now abandoned, the last crop unharvested. Several seasons ago, he thought.

He recognized it at once with a quickening of excitement. It was one of the places he had seen or dreamed he had seen or which had been described to him while he was under the influence of Martagón's sacred drug in the tipi in the woods above Taos pueblo. It was the place where the voices had told him he would find the end of his Peyote Road.

The three riders descending the break in the arroyo wall reached the bottom and rode on upstream again through the dry stalks of unshucked corn. Jaime returned to the mare, remounted, and continued along the rim.

The meander of the arroyo presently turned back on itself and the ruins of a considerable establishment came into view. A dam, now long ruptured and dry, had been raised across the stream threading the arroyo floor. A diversion ditch led from one end of this to the race of a mill which was now a burned out shell, roofless and half melted back into the red adobe earth from which it had been raised. Attached were the remnant walls of a large building which had also once been a manufactory of some sort.

Immediately below the dam was a stout house, backed up protectively against its base. Surrounding the house were the shells of half a dozen smaller buildings which Jaime judged to have been additional living quarters and the various service buildings necessary to such an ambitious enterprise in this remote place. All had also been burned out, but most of the roof of the house was intact, the door was still hung, and the window openings had been securely boarded up within.

Further downstream were extensive corrals and some stock sheds which had escaped fire damage but appeared equally abandoned. Jaime's excitement quickened further. Martagón's voices had not showed him this in the peyote tipi, but he thought Father Frederico had tried to do so, at least insofar as a hunch could go. A place of death, the padre had said. They would be safe in hiding there. From discovery by Indians and Mexican *paisanos* alike. Both would shun a place where men had died, superstitiously fearing the spirits remaining.

This was such a place. Jaime knew now what place it was. The ruins of Simeon Turley's farm and mills and distillery. The home of Taos Lightning, the famous and redoubtable mountain-man whiskey which had once traveled the length and breadth of the high country and now could no longer be had. And the settlement he had seen in the distance on down the stream on the trade trail was the old Spanish village known as Arroyo Hondo.

In the uprising which had cost Governor Charlie Bent and other territorial officers their lives and Father Frederico his old mission at Taos, Turley and his staff had been burned out and murdered here through the treachery of a friend. This was all that remained of half a lifetime of hard and ingenious labor. That and the ghosts of the dead.

Before men appeared in the open below, Jaime knew he had found Helga Cagle. If she yet lived.

They came from the ruins like rabbits from burrows of a warren as the three he had been paralleling approached. A dozen men. Even at this distance he recognized among them those he had been shown by the peyote voices. A thin, gray, lightly moving Yankee who wore two guns. An Indian from somewhere on down the valley of the Rio Grande.

And the leader. This one impressed Jaime most, as

he had in the vision. A tall man, powerful and hand-some, at least in part Indian, himself, as Lela Archu-leta had promised he might be, reading only from the tracks she and Ramón had followed to the forks of the Cimarroncito.

Espada, the voices had said. The Ace of Spades.

There should have been a black man, also, as Jaime remembered it, but he was not visible among them as they moved out to meet the three who were coming in. From his vantage Jaime could hear the sound if not the words of their challenge and the response of the newcomers. But there was no sign of a woman. Noth-ing to assure him Helga was still with them.

He waited impatiently, knowing he did not dare ex-pose himself. Probably not until dark gave him fair odds at attempting to move in closer. A long time yet.

Espada sent the thin, gray man into the house on the double. The rest waited with Espada for the trio's approach. Espada drew his gun, but the whole group seemed only wary, not hostile. Nor were the newcom-ers, to all appearances. They dismounted. Espada ges-tured them toward the house with his weapon. They, too, disappeared within and Espada closed the door behind him as he followed, leaving the rest of his men in the dooryard.

They idled there for some minutes, apparently awaiting the outcome of whatever colloquy was being held within the house. It came, suddenly, in the form of two almost simultaneous gunshots behind the closed door of the ruined *casa*. The sound galvanized the men in the yard. They bunched uncertainly. The door was almost immediately opened to them and they entered.

A few more brief moments ensued which Jaime was forced to endure in curious, concerned impatience. Then they filed back out, obviously under orders. The foremost carried the limp bodies of the trio which had led him here. The cover was removed from a well in

the dooryard and the dead were unceremoniously
dumped into it. Jaime swore softly at this. In this dry
country, deliberate fouling of any water supply was
one of the few cardinal sins recognized by all. But it
told him Espada did not intend to remain here long,
whatever the justification for the death of the three
from the south.

The men in the yard scattered quickly to their burrows among the ruins and to the sheds at the corrals,
dragging out gear and leading horses out into view to
saddle up in what was plainly preparation for immediate departure. One unsaddled horse remained at the
sheds when the men there were through. Jaime saw
with a quick lift of hope that it was the Corona mount
Helga had ridden back from the banks of the Cimarroncito with him. But the hope ebbed as poles were
kicked down and the animal was turned free.

As they came back up from the corrals, some of the
men cut the girths and headstalls on the dead men's
dusty horses, letting the tack lie as it fell and freeing
them, as well. Saddled and geared up, Espada's men re-
gathered before the house and one went to the door to
summon those within. Jaime tensed, knowing he
would discover now whether they still held their prisoner from the Corona or not.

They filed out. All of them but the thin, gray man
who had been wearing two guns at his belt. The last
was the black man Jaime had expected but had not
seen. He carried a small, tarp-wrapped bundle which
he fastened to the roll of gear others had lashed to his
cantle for him.

They swung up and rode through the breach in the
dam and on up the arroyo toward the timber reaching
down from the north slope of the heavily wooded Taos
mountain. Behind them, one saddled horse remained
at the rail before the ruins of Simeon Turley's house.
But the man with the two belted guns did not reap-
pear. There was no sign of Helga Cagle.

Jaime quickly returned to the Corona mare, remounted, and rode back at a full run toward the break in the rim which offered the only practical descent to the arroyo floor that he had seen. Before a twist of the deeply scoured watercourse might obscure them, he looked back upstream. Espada and his file of men, with the black man bringing up the rear and lagging a little, were riding briskly toward the first timber at the head of the arroyo. The man with the two belt guns had not rejoined them.

Jaime did not remember the detour back to the rimbreak as so long and he rode recklessly, crowding the mare. The horse took the break when they reached it without slackening or a falter in stride, cascading earth and torn sod ahead as they went down in great, sliding plunges, cutting across the more patient switchbacks of the little used and poorly marked trail to the bottom. Once onto the formerly cultivated bench beside the streambed, they cut across the lazy meanders as well, sending the remnant standing stalks of long dry, unharvested corn flying.

The doubling back had taken only a few minutes in all. Less than half an hour at most. But when Jaime rounded the reverse turn obscuring the Turley place, he saw that another was before him. Riding as hard as Jaime himself, the black man who had brought up the rear of Espada's departing file hammered through the rupture in the old mill dam, reining back hard as he came into the yard to approach the house more cautiously and quietly.

Jaime was just passing the corrals, two hundred yards downstream, when the man swung down beside the remaining saddled horse at the rail and darted through the doorway. That remaining distance seemed interminable. As Jaime vaulted down beside the other two horses, gun leaping to hand, the black man came running from the house with Helga limp in his arms.

Jaime saw that her face was brutally bruised and swollen and that she was unconscious or nearly so. The man carrying her froze in blank astonishment as he saw Jaime.

"Holy sainted Mother of the good Lord, Himself," he breathed, "I'd sworn Sloane killed you dead!"

"Put her down, you black bastard," Jaime ordered raggedly. "Gently, damn you!"

Helga's eyes fluttered open at the sound of his voice and widened incredulously in spite of the swelling about them. Tears streamed from them and she started to struggle as the man holding her tried to obey Jaime's order.

"Jaime!" she sobbed. "Oh, God, Jaimie!"

Her feet touched the ground, but she was too unsteady to stand unaided and she had to cling to the black man. Jaime stepped forward to swing her away from the son of a bitch for a clean shot and she saw the gun in his hand, hammer back at full cock.

"No, Jaime, no!" she gasped. "He came back to help me when I thought—when I thought there wasn't anybody else."

Fury shaking him at the pain in her swollen features, Jaime gripped her arm purposefully, but she clung more tightly to the black man.

"Look inside," she begged with an involuntary shudder. "That's what he saved me from."

The words made no sense but something Jaime suddenly realized did. Her dress had been half torn off and the shirt she had it covered with was the one the man with the twin belt-guns had been wearing when he disappeared into the house. Jaime freed her and turned toward the door. The black man clutched at him with his free hand.

"No time for that," he protested. "Or much of anything else, mister."

Jaime struck the hand away with the barrel of his gun.

"We'll make time," he said harshly.

He stepped into the ruined house to face a gutted main room with a smaller one off the far end. In the doorway between the two lay the shirtless body of the man with two belted guns. He lay on his face and there was a great, dark contusion at the base of his neck where it had been broken by a tremendous blow from some heavy blunt instrument.

He lifted the guns from a stool. One chamber of each had been fired. The smell of freshly burned powder clung to them. He thrust them into his own belt and ran back outside, holstering his own weapon. The black man had Helga at the dead man's horse and was trying to hoist her into the saddle.

"Damn it, can't you see she's in no shape to sit her own seat?" Jaime demanded.

"She'll have to," the black man said. "I had to wait till we got into timber before I could risk turning back with some hope they wouldn't notice for a spell. But they've had hell's aplenty time, now, and then some. They'll come rarin' back down here like Old Man Devil with a fire on his tail. And that'll be it, mister, for sure."

Jaime jerked the man's own horse around and indicated the saddle.

"Get up. I'll lift her up before you."

The man obeyed, pushing his roll and the tarp-wrapped bundle atop it back to make room for his thighs under the cantle. Jaime heaved Helga up to him. Silent, aware of the urgency, she helped as much as she could, her eyes on Jaime speaking things for which there were neither words nor time.

"Head around the next turn for a break in the south wall that'll take you to the rim," Jaime ordered.

"I know the place."

"Fast and don't look back. Head up the mountain into the nearest timber. I'll be with you before you get there."

"We'll still need Sloane's horse."

"Not if it can't be ridden—and have them know there's three of us when they'll only be expecting two? Damn it, go!"

Jaime clouted the rump of the man's horse. It jumped out and the man kicked it up to a full run, racing back down past the corrals. Jaime knew the animal could not keep the pace long with its double burden, but the important thing now was to get out of the trap formed by this arroyo without being seen.

He quickly slipped bridle and saddle from the horse belonging to the dead man in the house and also rump-slapped it on its way, hoping it would go far enough on its own to escape attention. There was a rifle in the boot. He transferred it swiftly to his own saddle.

He broke open the dead man's roll of gear and found shot, caps, and powder for the belt guns he had lifted and the rifle. He thrust them into his shirt for now and lugged saddle, bridle, and gear to the well in the yard, dumping them in atop the dead.

Running back to the mare, he swung up in a flying mount and was on his way. When he reached the turn obscuring Turley's, he looked back. The dam blocked part of the view up the arroyo, but Espada and his men were not in sight. And if they couldn't be seen, neither could he. It seemed fair enough exchange, for now. Time enough to close with them later and settle the Corona's score along with Helga's when he had her clear and safe. It was a big country and Espada and his defecting black man weren't the only ones who knew how to double back on a trail.

In a few more minutes he put the mare to the slant of the break toward the arroyo rim. Helga and the black man had just disappeared over the lip above on their already laboring horse. The mare seemed to understand the urgency and made almost as short work of the ascent as she had the slide down. At the top he pulled up to look back. Turley's abandoned corn fields were as empty as when he had first seen them. So they had gained that advantage and held it.

Knowing that they were now invisible from below, Jaime rode on toward the timber into which Helga and the black man had already disappeared.

# CHAPTER 14

Jaime followed the tracks of the black man's doubly laden horse and found it not as easy as he expected. But there was compensation. It would slow any behind as well. He was nearly a mile into the timber before he overtook Helga and her rescuer.

He passed them without pulling up, signaling them to follow him in turn, and quickly outdistanced them on ahead. It would have pleased him to be able to hide their signs of passage, but at the moment, time was more important.

He worked rapidly toward higher ground, clinging to the advantage of superior elevation, and came presently to what he hoped to find—an open tongue of sidehill grass snaking up through the heavy pine growth. From the upper edge of this he had a view back to a portion of the Arroyo Hondo rim. He located Espada and his men at once. They had just emerged from the break leading to the bottom and were fanning out in search of sign as they rode toward first timber.

Jaime saw that he and his companions had gained a little better lead than he expected, and he was grateful. But they were close. Too close. Twenty minutes at the best, in terms of time. There could be no stopping, yet, no way to look to Helga or even to talk. Even a few hundred yards were important, now.

He carefully counted those below because that also was important. To know the odds precisely. There

were eleven of them. One lay dead in the ruins of the
Turley house. Another was with Helga. And Helga,
herself. So Lela Archuleta's count of fourteen on the
Cimarroncito had been accurate. And she had not
counted individuals, only the marks they left behind.

He marvelled again at the instinctive skill most Indians seemed to possess. Merely a commonsense business of remembering precisely how nature looked undisturbed and alertly watching for anything out of
place. So his friend Chato of the Utes had once told
him. But to Jaime it was sometimes uncanny, no matter how hard he tried to practice it himself.

As he watched below, he had a sharp reminder this
advantage lay with Espada now. The leader and the
shorter Indian with him, the one Jaime had judged
was from one of the lower Rio Grande villages, cutting
close together, simultaneously picked up the tracks of
the two horses. Espada signaled the others. They
bunched together again and came on, eagerly kicking
up their own mounts. Jaime wheeled the mare and
rode back in his own tracks to meet Helga and the
black man.

Reining alongside their laboring horse, he extended
an arm to Helga. With the black man's help she transferred to his saddle as he shifted back over the cantle
to give her room in the seat before him. He steadied
her with his free arm and she leaned against him,
grateful for the support.

The mare snorted softly at the added burden but
picked up willingly at the touch of the boot. The black
man's horse, relieved of her weight, responded as well.
They rode on steadily upslope, threading the thick
stand of pine and spruce at a better pace.

Jaime kept his eyes ahead, watching the changing
shape of the mountain as they ascended, looking back
only when it seemed possible a vantage might be afforded or there was some risk of exposing themselves
to view from below. He was anxious to keep their pursuit slowed to following the tracks of the two horses

alone, without direct visual contact if at all possible.

The third or fourth time Helga felt him turn, her own body stiffened a little.

"Still following?"

"Like dogs after a three-legged coyote."

"You sure?"

"Too damned sure for comfort. Rest, if you can. You're going to need it."

"We mustn't lose them, Jaime."

"Fat chance, riding double like this."

"We mustn't let them give up."

"They won't."

She sighed a little and leaned back against him again, seemingly content on that point, at least. It made little sense to Jaime, but he let it lie, doubting that she was in any shape for coherence yet. But in a few minutes she stirred anxiously again, obviously struggling for clarification but able to deal with only one random thought at a time.

"Where are Spence and the crew?" she asked. "We've got to warn them. As quick as we can. How far is it to where you left them?"

"Far as the Corona. That's where they are. That's where they'll stay. I hope."

She twisted sharply then to look at him with almost as much incredulity as when she first saw him in Turley's dooryard.

"You came alone?"

"Oh, Spence raised hell. So did Raul and the boys. 'Mana, too, at first. But that was the way it had to be. The only way. Don't worry about it, now. I'm here, anyway."

She faced front and leaned against him once again.

"Yes. Yes, you're here. And I thought you were dead."

"Just a sore head and a sudden bald patch. 'Mana's first-rate at patching a man up, but a damned poor hand at barbering."

"I'm so glad, Jaime. So glad."

She lapsed into silence. In a little while he thought by her weight that she slept.

He worked them along an upward-slanting sidehill to a heavily wooded ravine creasing the flank of the mountain. Running water rose to meet them there. The black man understood at once, at least in part, and reined into the stream, intending to ride up it against the current.

"Downstream," Jaime ordered sharply.

"Let them get above us and they'll cut us off someplace between here and the top," the man protested. "No good giving them any ground we don't have to."

"That's what they'll figure. So we'll go down a ways and leave no tracks. What ground we'll lose we'll gain in time while they look for where we came out of the water up above."

The black man shrugged with obvious disapproval but obediently reined the other way. Jaime rode the mare into the stream and they rode with its current.

In about half a mile, as Jaime had noted in setting their course, one bank of the ravine became a spur which petered out to nothing at a junction with a heavily wooded water-bearing ravine cutting down the side of the mountain. Disapproval suddenly gone, the black man turned without order up this second watercourse, staying to the bed of the stream.

Jaime noted the man's quick grasp of essentials in work like this and his sensible avoidance of unnecessary talk or questions. A plan began to take shape in his mind. He elaborated upon it as they rode steadily up this second creek, gaining altitude again and secure in the knowledge that they now had the intervening spur between them and their pursuit and a dead end ahead, somewhere above, which Espada and his men would have to unravel before they could pick up the trail of their quarry again.

The streambed was not as rocky as some, but it was

markedly slower and harder going for the horses than the banks would have been. Nevertheless, as his plan continued to develop in his mind, Jaime became more convinced they could afford to risk tiring the animals this early to gain further advantage. For this reason, he kept them to water so that all marks of passage continued to be erased as they were made.

Once, the horse ahead lifted its tail to loose droppings, some of which landed on an exposed rock. The black man dismounted at once and kicked the manure into the water. It diluted and washed away to nothing with the rest and he scrubbed the rock clean before he remounted.

Presently the sun dipped behind timber on the spur ridge and shadows lengthened in the ravine. Jaime led them on up the streambed until the light became so poor that the horses began to stumble a little and it was folly to further risk cannon-bones on the wet and slippery footing of water-polished rocks.

He thought that Espada and his men, following the other creek on the far side of the intervening ridge in an attempt to find where they had emerged from water, would have realized by now that they had been tricked. It seemed unlikely at this hour that they would double back or cast wider to regain the lost trail until morning light.

He began to search the banks and shortly he rode out onto a patch of good grass on a little bench beside a long, quiet pool which the creek had scoured out against an outcropping stone ledge on the opposite bank. Fergy Ferguson, a devoted admirer of 'Mana Stanton and an occasional visitor at the Corona in the early days, had taught him this inflexible habit of always picking quiet water to stop beside along a mountain stream. Another of the fragments of recollected advice and personal experience which constituted the only real schooling he had ever received.

The old mountain man had pointed out that a rushing creek made more noise than a man realized, particularly if he had been traveling along it for some time, and his hearing had become unconsciously impaired. Beside a pool like this one, hearing sharpened and a traveler could sense even a quiet approach where he could not beside white water.

The black man dismounted, pulled his blanket roll from beneath the tarp-wrapped package on his cantle, and crossed to Jaime's stirrup. Jaime unlashed his own roll and handed it to him. The man spread the blankets in a comfortable place at the edge of the pool. Returning, he gently lifted Helga down. As they helped her to the blankets, a drift of breeze from the ridge brought them confirmation of Espada's intentions—the incomparable evening fragrance of a pitch-pine mountain supper fire.

Jaime knelt and dampened his kerchief to bathe Helga's face. She took it from him.

"Mind the horses," she said. "This is a woman's job. I can manage."

The black man appreciatively sniffed the smoke-scented air as Jaime joined him to unsaddle. He nodded toward the ridge.

"Right nice of them to let us know," he said.

"Yeah," Jaime agreed. "I hoped they'd night it where they were. But they must think we're farther away to light a fire. And I wish to hell we were so we could do the same. It's going to get colder'n billy-be-damned in this draw directly."

"Seems like," the black man agreed. "The missy better?"

Jaime nodded.

"She slept some, I think. Bastards sure beat the hell out of her."

"That was Espada. Gave her a be-jesus of a slapping around when he found out she'd been lying. I couldn't do a thing, the way it was right then."

Jaime hesitated, knowing he had to ask but afraid of the answer.

"That all?"

"Lucky for her," the black man agreed. "Wouldn't a been if Sloane'd got to her. He was supposed to finish her off when he was done. That's why I come back as soon as I could give 'em the slip. I'm a no-good black son of a bitch, mister. That's a fact. But I had to."

Sloane. Jaime remembered the name written across the face of a dog-eared ace of spades which had been found beneath the misused body of a young Indian girl lying dead with two others in the grass of a mountain meadow. He thought that Martagón and his followers of the Peyote Road would be satisfied to know that their prayers had been answered. That violent death had come again to disturb the spirits haunting the ruins of Turley's mill.

They would be a damned sight better satisfied before Jaime Henry finished his job and was ready to head back toward the Corona. So, he thought, would even the old *cacique* of the Taos pueblos. His people would have justice without risk of involvement with alien Yankee authority, and he could lift his ban.

The peyote eaters could return from penance at their spirit lake. The names of grived-for dead could be spoken again among the bereaved families and the rest of the pueblo.

Those who had laid hands to Helga Cagle would lay hands to no others. And in Santa Fe ambitious plotters yet nameless would learn in due time that no man could strike at the Stantons and their ranch or those who lived and worked upon it without full and merciless retaliation.

"I'm beholden," he said to the black man, extending his hand. "The name's Jim Henry. Jaime, they call me. I ride *segundo* for the Stantons."

The man looked across at Helga, now lying on blankets with Jaime's kerchief a cold compress on her bruised face.

"I know," he said. "She told us when we all thought Sloane had knocked you out of saddle dead center. He didn't often miss. She thinks mine's Huggo. But that was Sloane, too. He was always ragging at me, any way he could. Here's the way my mammy had the preacher write it in her Book."

He fumbled out a playing card like the one Martagón had showed Jaime beside the old game trail across from the Cimarroncito. Jaime read the letters hand-printed across the pips.

"Hugo?"

"That's the right of it. You tell the missy and see to her. I got a little chore." He gestured off toward the source of the smoke from beyond the ridge. "They maybe got a fire, yonder, but they ain't going to feed as good as we are. Ain't more'n a few grits among the lot. We'll do a sight better."

He started to open his tarp-wrapped parcel as Jaime recrossed to Helga. She removed the damp kerchief from her face and sat up as she felt him settle beside her. He saw that cleansed and with even this brief application of cold creek water, swelling seemed to have receded a little and her appearance was much improved. Maybe it was only that fear was gone, but she seemed herself again.

She took off his hat, examined the wound scarring his shorn scalp, and insisted upon bathing it for him, a gentle ministration which said much without words. Looking at her, Jaime felt a fresh rush of gratitude toward Hugo and an envy at the same time. He would have greatly liked the satisfaction of leaving his own mark on the man named Sloane. But Espada yet remained. And the others. He would get to them presently.

He told Helga about Hugo's name and showed her the card with it printed upon it.

"I liked Huggo," she protested mischievously. "The more I saw of him, the more I was tempted. He was absolutely beautiful when he broke that bloodless stud's neck!"

Presently Hugo joined them. He spread his piece of

tarp before them as he might cloth on a table. A heap of thin strips of rich, fire-cured beef jerky lay upon it. Enough, Jaime saw with considerable relief, to last them for several days. He had been concerned about food. Hugo emptied his hat beside the jerky, mounding up a pile of sweet red mountain currants from a nearby thicket.

"You going to do the honors like my mammy used to, Missy?" the black man asked with a grin.

To his surprise as well as Jaime's, Helga caught the nearest hand of each, closed her eyes, and lowered her head.

"Praise the Lord, from Whom all blessings flow," she murmured in a soft, suddenly husky voice. "If I knew how to say more, I would."

Jaime saw tears course from under her closed lashes.

"Hell's bells," he growled uncomfortably, "let's eat. I'm hungry."

# CHAPTER 15

When they had eaten, Jaime listened, probing with an occasional sharp question, while Helga and Hugo told him all that had happened since he had been shot from saddle—all that they knew or thought important about Espada, his nameless employers, and his intentions. As he listened, the plan which had been shaping in his mind while they rode took form. It was, he knew, time for them to separate.

He indicated Helga.

"She trusts you so I'll have to," he told Hugo.

"You can," the black man said. "I sure ain't going back where I come from—if I want to stay living. You say it; I'll do it. Or bust a gut trying."

"We'll get some sleep for a couple of hours, then move out before they're stirring over the ridge yonder. Horses'll have to be led till there's light, but you can climb a saddle if you begin to play out, Helga."

"I'll manage," she said in sharp defense.

"Sure," he agreed with a grin. "We all will. Best bet's to head on up the mountain to that saddle we saw off east at sunset. The trade road from Taos over to cut the Santa Fe Trail's got to be up there beyond it, somewhere. Once over the divide, it'll be an easy run home down the Cimarron canyon."

"But that's the way Espada's going to go," Helga protested. "What if he decides not to waste any more time looking for us? I don't think we're that important to him. Only the Corona is. And I tell you he'll kill them all to get his hands on it!"

"That's his way," Hugo agreed. "He knows that business good."

"What if he decides to head there direct, Jaime? We won't stand a chance of getting there first, riding double and all."

"You won't be riding double," Jaime said quietly. "Spence's mare is yours from here on. I won't be needing a horse for what I have to do. I don't have that far to go."

Helga was puzzled for a moment, then as she began to understand, her swollen features set in stubborn, exasperated refusal.

"Oh, for Christ's sake, Jaime!" she exploded. "Alone, afoot—against eleven men?"

"My job. What I get paid for. To buy you and Hugo enough time here to make it home and warn Spence in case I make a mistake or bite off a mite more than I can chew. With luck, to make sure to the last son of a bitch that the bastards never lay hands on another woman or trouble the Corona again."

"Sure, sure," Helga said scathingly. "Nothing to it. Jaime Henry, single-handed. You got to do everything like you make love? A bull loose in a heifer pen. All balls and no brains. You know what Spence Stanton would say to such a damned fool notion!"

Jaime winced at the reference and felt anger rise, but he checked it.

"Spence already had his say. But I'm here." He dropped a hand reassuringly to her knee. "Hell, it's no big thing. I've got two rifles and three handguns. That's five down without even reloading."

"That bullet didn't do you any good. *Segundo* doesn't mean God Almighty. Can't you get that through your thick head?"

"Advantage is with me. They think there's only the two of you. Once you're on your way, they won't even be able to figure out what the hell's happening until it's too late. For some of them, anyway. When I need a horse, there'll be empty saddles to choose from. I guarantee you that."

"No, God damn it! You were killed once. I shouldn't give a hoot in hell, but I do and I'm not going through that again. We leave here together or I stay, too."

Patience fraying, Jaime heaved irritably to his feet, mindful of the few times since he had joined her husband that 'Mana Stanton had seen fit to stand inflexibly against him in Spence's absence when the interests of the Corona and the lives of herself and others were at stake. He had not known then how to deal with a stubborn woman and he did not know now.

"You'll damned well do what you're told," he said harshly. "Both of you. Now turn in!"

Hugo rose unhurriedly to face him in the darkness.

"Reckon you're right, Jaime," the black man said. "Account of the people you work for, you can't risk letting Espada even start across the mountains for fear he might make it before we could. If he did, he'd kill. No other way with him. Or any of the rest, long as they've got the papers and the guns to back them up. So they got to be killed."

"You're as crazy as he is!" Helga accused, leaping up angrily.

Hugo ignored her.

"But the missy's right about how it's got to be done," he continued. "Three's better'n one, no matter how good that one thinks he is. Or what he thinks he's got to do. Even when one of the three's a woman. This one, anyhow. I'm staying, too."

"Like hell!" Jaime snapped, stiffening truculently.

Hugo shook his head, reading his thoughts before he was fully aware of them himself.

"You can't do it, Jaime," Hugo said. "Not with a gun. We both know we can't risk the sound. And I don't think you can do it with your hands. I wouldn't try. Not with me. Ask the missy. She saw Sloane die."

"I'm not Sloane."

"No. Nor God Almighty, like the missy said. Take my word for it or you may get bent up some. For your own good. Hers and mine. And the folks on the Corona."

Jaime was not misled by the softly sibilant tone or the gentleness of the warning. And he was acutely aware of the immense, lightly leashed physical power in the stocky figure before him. Perhaps it was these realizations which got to him. Perhaps it was an instinctive flash of belated better judgment, but his anger cooled. Tenseness ran from him and he chuckled.

"Never seen an outfit in such a spoil for a fight," he said. "Looks like I've been outvoted. How about some shuteye? We got a tolerable day's work coming up tomorrow."

Hugo put one great hand to his arm and gripped it.

"We'll get her done, boy," he promised.

"I don't trust either one of you," Helga said with an audible sniff.

She picked up the blankets on which they had earlier been sitting, intending to shake them out, then paused in sudden realization.

"Some trail hands! Two blankets for three of us."

"For you," Jaime corrected. "Hugo and I'll make do."

"Not and get some sleep," the black man said. "Any of us. Going to get too cold, directly. But there's a way—"

He paused and looked uncertainly at his companions.

"Nightstove, my mammy used to call it when we was all home and short of bed fixings in winter and no wood for the fire."

He paused again.

"Kind of cozy-like, but it works real good. One blanket under and one over and you in the middle, Missy. If you got no feeling about it."

Helga understood at once.

"Why should I?" she asked.

She spread the two blankets down on the grass, one atop the other, and slid between them in the middle of the bed thus made, turning the corners back invitationally on each side of her for the two men. Hugo hesitated until Jaime took his place beside Helga on one side without comment. Then the black man slid in on the other.

He chuckled softly after a moment.

"No offense, but I always wondered what it'd be like to sleep with a white woman. Never figured I'd find out this way."

Jaime felt him pin his corner of the blanket so the increasing chill could not penetrate. He put his belt-gun under cover as a chock against which he could roll in the night and did the same. Slowly, the heat of their bodies melded in comfort.

Jaime lay with his back toward Helga, waiting for sleep. On the other side of the girl, Hugo's breathing gradually slowed to a deep, regular rhythm and in a surprisingly short time, Jaime thought the black man slept. He envied the ease with which Hugo did so, seemingly ignoring the day behind and what might lie ahead and the ruthlessly purposeful men encamped in the next draw, no more than a mile or two away along the flank of the mountain.

Jaime had no such efficient control, himself. He thought few men did. He had known only one other, Spencer Stanton. He believed it must be an acquired ability, learned of many hard-pressed camps. A self-willed closing off of the mind with its plaguing, sleep-destroying thoughts, concerns, and uncertainties. A willing acceptance of present risk in order to refuel the body for more effective later effort.

Presently, to Jamie's relief, Helga seemed to drift off. He was pleased. Her ordeal was not over and she needed to regain as much strength as she could.

Some time later, he felt her stir slightly. Silently, slowly, she began to turn toward him, facing his back, with many small movements. Her hand tentatively sought him and slowly drew him tightly to her. Her fingers continued to gently knead the muscles of his chest, but all other movement stopped in seeming contentment at being closer to his heat.

But in a little while, when he was finally beginning to drop off himself, she whispered very softly into the back of his neck.

"Jaime?"

He tightened his muscles in response and her encircling arm hugged him closer. The faint whisper behind his ear came again.

"So much to say."

He listened for any interruption in the rhythm of Hugo's breathing. It continued without change and he whispered back.

"Tomorrow. Sleep, now."

"No. I may not get another chance. I know what that's like. I died when I thought you were dead. I have to say it."

Jaime listened again. Hugo's breathing remained unchanged. The sounds they made were very small, too soft to penetrate the depths in which the black man slept.

"All right," he told Helga. "I want to hear."

"I wished I had let you have me when you wanted," she whispered.

"I was afraid for you."

"Or what they might do to me?"

He rocked his head up and down a little in assent.

"Sloane would have killed me today, when he was finished, if Hugo hadn't come back. But not before. Not when they thought I was 'Mana Stanton. He just wanted me on my back. That's all he gave a damn about. I could see it in his eyes from the start. And he would have, too, if Espada hadn't kept him away from me."

The whisper stopped. Helga waited. Jaime made no response. Her whisper resumed.

"You should have seen what he did to that child—that Indian girl. In front of us all."

"I did."

"Would it have made any difference if he had to me? Like he wanted. Any difference, now? To you? If they all had?"

Jaime's answer came with more stress than he intended.

"How the hell do I know?"

The whisper seemed loud enough to echo. Both lay rigid, waiting, but Hugo's breathing continued its regular rhythm. In a few moments, Jaime continued carefully.

"I can't answer that. No man can. Until it happens. Because he doesn't know. Enough talk, now."

"Why?"

"Because you aren't saying what you mean to say. That's all I want to hear. Forget the rest. I've had enough of it."

There was a long pause. Helga's body moved ever so slightly and her hand tightened against his chest. It was like a total caress.

"Yes," she whispered. "So have I. Thank God. I lied to you before. Because I couldn't say it. Some kind of pride, I guess. Some woman thing I didn't understand."

"Say it now," Jaime urged softly.

"I wanted Spence Stanton, once. Or thought I did. You know that, I suppose. But I never wanted him—I never wanted anything—like I wanted you. Like I want you, now."

"Then say it, God damn it. Say it right out."

There was a pause as though she was summoning determination to do a difficult thing. Then the whisper came again, so softly he could barely hear it.

"I love you, Jaime Henry."

He smiled broadly in the darkness. Some things a man just plain had to start right. His hand moved up to cover hers on his chest.

"That's better," he said approvingly.

"I want to show you, Jaime."

"With three in a bed?"

The little movement of her body came again and his answered.

"We can pretend," she whispered. "All night. Maybe tomorrow, somewhere—"

His hand moved to her upturned thigh in response.

Jaime roused sometime before first light to find that he had slept well and was refreshed. Hugo was already at the horses, saddling silently. Helga was beside him, smiling as he sat up. She also seemed rested. He thought most of the swelling was gone from her bruised features. A well-blackened eye was the only mark of her mistreatment at Espada's hands. And there was luminescence in her smile, as though they had indeed made love through the night.

Hugo's back was momentarily to them. Jaime leaned over and kissed her. Lips opened hungrily and those two dew-dampened blankets on creek-bank grass became a very difficult bed to leave.

They ate in the graying dark and made up their saddle rolls in silence. Each was acutely aware that the larger camp in the next draw might also be astir or even in motion, although Jaime noted with satisfaction that there was no trace of smoke from a breakfast fire on the air.

Gear was up and Jaime was helping Helga into the saddle on the Corona mare, preparatory to leading out afoot, when Hugo spoke casually from the head of his own horse.

"Don't know if you fellows realize it or not," the black man said with a carefully straight face, "but you talk in your sleep."

# CHAPTER 16

When light improved sufficiently, they mounted, Jaime with Helga riding double before him. It was his intention to follow the draw in which they had nighted until it headed out, somewhere further up the mountain. Once out on the mountain flank, he thought they could find a place which also commanded the head of the stream in which Espada's party had camped. In this way they could set up a suitable ambush when pursuit appeared, whichever of the two draws it followed.

However, they discovered their creek headed against the sheer wall of a box canyon from which there was no practical way out except the way they had come. They had to retrace their steps a considerable distance, risking encounter with those who might now be following closely, before Jaime could find a sidehill climb possible for the horses. It took better than half an hour to work up around the head of the box canyon onto the unbroken flank of the mountain again. There, with the first low-slanted shafts of the sun in their faces, they found tracks. They were fresh, hastily and carelessly made, and there could be no misreading them.

Espada and his men had apparently broken camp about the same time that they had, probably also leading their horses until light improved sufficiently and continuing on up the draw in which they had camped. But unlike their own, it must have tapered out as it climbed without a headwall to enforce a detour. As a result, those they hunted and who had been hunting them had crossed above them while they were fighting up out of the box canyon and were now ahead instead of behind as had been intended.

Hugo thought it was merely an accident of terrain and that when no evidence of their own passage was encountered, Espada would shortly pull up to cast about for sign, backtracking when none could be found. If they kept higher up the slope, they should be able to spot and approach with time to pick their ground and set their ambush.

Jaime wanted to agree, but he could not. He feared that as Helga had phophesied, Espada, having lost them the night before, had given up the search and intended to drive straight for the Corona before any warning could reach the ranch ahead of him. Instead of concern over staying ahead of pursuit until a proper place and circumstances to make a stand could be found, Jaime was afraid that mounted as they were, they could not overtake Espada's force, now that it was ahead of them.

Helga shared his fears. Hugo accepted his judgment but was not so concerned.

"If you're right, they'll ride fast but take the easy way," the black man said. "To save their horses because they got a long way to go and'll want 'em fit for fighting when they get there. Means they'll take that saddle yonder that we was going to head for. But the shortest way and the quickest is right over the top of the mountain. May ga'nt our own horses some. And us. But we can be waiting for them when they hit that trade road on the other side."

Jaime looked at the mountain towering high above them and nodded reluctantly. There was no other way to save the time they needed. If Espada was driving for the trail from Taos to the headwaters of the Cimarron, as now seemed certain, there might be some chance of intercepting him. But it would be hard going and any mischance which caused further delay would render the effort useless.

With considerable misgiving, Jaime nudged the mare. They rode across Espada's tracks and lined straight upslope toward the distant summit above.

The summit of Taos mountain was easier gained than appeared from below. Scarcely a quarter of a mile straight up the slope from where they had crossed the fresh tracks of Espada's party, Jaime, Helga, and Hugo struck a narrow but well-worn Indian trail reaching upward from the apparent direction of the adobe village at Arroyo Hondo or some similar point of departure considerably downstream from the ruins of the Turley place.

Jaime saw with satisfaction that it was no simple evolution from a natural game trail, as such other tracks he had encountered on this side of the Sangre de Cristos had been. This one had been carefully laid out, a way cut through at considerable labor, where necessary, so that it kept altogether to the cover of deep timber and left no telltale scar of passage on the mountain.

It climbed steadily, but at a grade Jaime thought had been deliberately calculated to avoid pulls which would unduly break the wind of a good horse. In many stretches, it could be ridden at an easy lope. The Corona mare, even doubly laden, worked smoothly, without blowing. And Hugo's mount showed no distress.

Jaime presently became convinced that like the second emergency tunnel which was a part of every prairie-dog warren, this track was a secret approach or escape route established by the Indians in case of threat or necessity to cross the mountain rapidly and unseen, and he wondered what its destination was.

Where a granite spur thrust up through the trees above them, Jaime transferred Helga to the black man's horse and put his own to the detritus slope, climbing high enough to have a view out over the tops of screening timber. The notch over to the east was in plain view. In a few moments, lining directly for it, he spotted movement. Espada's party rode into the open, crossing a bald patch of grass.

They were some miles distant, now, and two or three thousand feet below. They were riding steadily, making their own trail for the notch, but at no great effort toward haste. It seemed possible that Hugo had been right; they were conserving their horses against need for mobility and a fast strike when they reached the Corona.

It also seemed likely that when both groups topped their respective summits and started down toward the Taos trade road, he and his two companions would have regained some advantage. But it could again be as easily lost. And if some fluke of accident or terrain permitted Espada and his men to rebuild a lead, there would be no way to warn the ranch ahead of them.

Fretting at this stubbornly recurrent realization, Jaime dropped back to the Indian trail and overtook Hugo and Helga. They looked anxiously at him. His best answer was a shrug. He told them what he had seen and let it go at that, without the speculation which was troubling him.

He would have the situation other than it was if he could. He would have liked to draw Espada's men after them, further away from the Corona, rather than toward it, eager in the belief they were tracking only Hugo and the girl he had rescued, until a trap could be devised and sprung and Espada could be dealt with on this side of the mountains, ending at a distance any threat to the Stantons and their ranch. But he and Helga and the black man were in no better position to invite pursuit than to pursue.

Almost imperceptibly, rounding like a gentle knoll, the summit of Taos Mountain passed under them and they found themselves slanting downward in the warmer sun of the south slope. By some accident of wind and soil and the lie of winter snow, timber growth was no less vigorous but much thinner here, with many small, aspen-fringed parks, interspersed with granite outcroppings.

Shortly they began to catch intermittent glimpses of the Taos trade road which climbed over the spine of the Sangre de Cristos to the headwaters of the Cimarron and down to eventual junction with the Santa Fe Trail out on the *llanos* east of the Corona. There was no visible sign of traffic. Jaime could not make up his mind whether this was a boon or a further misfortune.

It was Hugo who spotted Espada's men, three or four miles to the east, starting down from the notch which they had crossed there. They were higher, now, for having made a long loop to the notch, but with a downslope ahead of them and more open going, they were riding more briskly, now.

Jaime saw at once that going directly over the mountain had not won them as much advantage as he had hoped. It was apparent both parties would reach the trade road at about the same time. He kicked up the mare and changed course, to cut the distance between them as much as he could, thinking that at worst he could make the single-handed stand he had earlier proposed here, hopefully buying Hugo and Helga Cagle time to get away and into the clear ahead of Espada.

Presently, through a vee in the folded hills across the narrow valley into which they were descending, a beautiful little hanging bowl containing a small lake came into view. Jaime recognized it as the sacred blue water of the *Taoseños*, which he had seen from the opposite side, coming down from the awesome heights of El Cumbre.

For an instant he thought that if they failed to reach or check Espada on the road below, they might be able to cross and drive straight south for the great pass with a fair chance of making the eastern slope of the mountains and the Corona ahead of Espada, who would be slowed by the longer if easier route down the Cimarron.

But almost as though the thought had mysteriously communicated itself, he felt a familiar pulsation, seemingly within his own body, and he knew distant drums were talking again from the opposite hills in which the little lake lay. They did not speak intelligibly, as they had in the *peyote* lodge, but their meaning was clear to Jaime.

Martagón and his friends were still there, doing penance to the ancient gods beside the blue lake. Maybe many others, as well. The intruders had been seen. Likely both parties, and the warning was the same for one as the other. That was a sacred place up there. Strangers would not be allowed a close approach, let alone to cross it. That was the law.

Jaime's spurt of hope died. To circle around the lake at the required distance for an approach to El Cumbre from this direction would cancel out any time gained in attempting the forbidding heights of the pass.

He glanced at his companions, but if either was aware of the drums, they gave no sign, and he began to wonder if they existed only in his imagination as some residual effect on the strange ritual fruit he had eaten in Taos. But he was convinced enough that the existence of the warning drumbeat was not something he wanted to put to a test.

He held on down into the valley, riding as fast as he dared without unduly inviting the attention of Espada and his men. Suddenly, when they were still several hundred yards above the road, slanting down parallel to it, Espada's party burst from an aspen thicket onto the track at no more than half a mile's distance. They pulled up abruptly there, knotted tight and milling for a moment.

Curious, Jaime did likewise, signaling Hugo to a stop beside Helga and himself. Espada and his men

continued to mill a moment longer in some kind of in-
decision or council, then kicked up their horses again.
Strangely they did not ride away, eastward, toward
the Moreno Valley and the easy passage through the
mountains to the headwaters of the Cimarron. Instead,
they came straight toward Jaime and his companions,
as though heading back to Taos.

It was only then that Jaime saw the Indians. They
were not many in any one place, two's and three's,
only, but they were in many places on both sides of
the road beyond Espada's oncoming group. They were
making no overtly hostile moves and showed themselves only enough for awareness of their presence
without affording the intruders targets worth the ex-
penditure of powder and ball. They were armed with
short, stout bows and the drums were among them,
warning loudly, now.

It was they who had turned Espada back, uncertain
of what he faced. He also had understood the talking
drums and obeyed them. Helga tapped Jaime's
shoulder and pointed behind them, down the road toward Taos. More moving shadows were in the timber
on both sides of the road.

Jaime searched the other side of the road. No movement was visible in timber and brush in that direction
—the direction of the sacred Blue Lake. Suddenly
Jaime thought he understood. As Espada and his oncoming men disappeared on a turn of the road which
obscured them, he kicked the mare up and rode
straight down the brief remaining slope to the road.
They crossed it and were into opposite cover before
Espada and his men reappeared.

Both Helga and Hugo were surprised by this sudden, unexpected dash and Jaime knew it, but there
was no time to explain. What was important to him
was that the warning drums were now behind and
were no longer talking to them. Martagón would not
fight—could not, as before—but he and his men were

doing what they could without becoming actually involved in confrontation, themselves.

Jaime held the mare straight up the opposite wall of the valley, brutally punishing her now under her double load and paying scant attention to cover. If he understood the boxing Indian lines and the message of the drums correctly, distance was the critical factor at this point—neither too much of a lead nor too little.

If they could achieve this balance of distance, he thought that being seen, even too briefly for adequate identification, might have value, if only to whet Espada into headlong pursuit. Every mile he rode after them here was a mile further from the attack he had planned on the Stanton's ranch.

On a little bench formed by the first rollback of the hills on this side of the valley and the trade road threading its floor, Jaime pulled up abruptly to wait for Hugo and his laboring mount to overtake them. Below, Espada's party became aware of the second shadowy, flitting line of Indians between them and further detour back toward Taos. They paused indecisively again. The leader's wily Comanche blood surfaced as he saw the fresh tracks of two horses cutting across the trail at a full run.

Although their lead was still dangerously scant and he knew he could have misread the Indian intent completely, Jaime slid one of the rifles from beneath his thigh and put a shot down into the knot of Espada's men. It was at extreme range and down-hill shooting, besides, but a horse or man was hit. He could not tell which. Only that the rider was nearly unseated, recovering only with the help of a companion.

The shot had the desired effect. Espada took the bait. He put his horse eagerly to the slope, shouting for his men to follow.

Jaime knew it was Hugo's blood that Espada scented. The black blood he hated in his own veins. The blood of a lesser man who had deserted him and rescued a woman who had lied him to within an ace of disaster. Personal affronts which the Comanche would give his eye teeth to see expiated in full. Even possession of the Corona could wait upon this—if the wait was not too long.

Obviously Espada was determined that it would not be, now that he had picked up the fugitives' trail again. But he did not yet realize that his real quarry and his most dangerous enemy was not the woman or the turncoat black man but another who rode with them without leaving a trace of his presence. The tracks he now followed, fresh as they were, could not lie. There were only two horses.

Jaime took what satisfaction he could from that thought, but it came in mighty scant measure and was a damned thin thread upon which to dangle the lives most precious to him, including his own, and the duty he owed the Stantons and Rancho Corona. He began to believe Helga had been right, back in the night camp. He might be Spencer Stanton's *segundo* and her lover, but he sure as hell wasn't God, whatever his convictions, vanities, and fancied abilities.

He had been caught like this a time or two at cards, probably through the same over-notion of his luck and the length of his own shadow, and he'd had to take his licks for it. But this wasn't a game. There was no folding this hand, now. The whole pot was on the table.

The Indian drums had faded out and there was no sound from below, but Jaime knew Espada was there, climbing toward them. Even if he had lost their unmistakable tracks, he would not quit this soon. Not after that shot. He knew he had bet too fast and baited too strong.

They climbed to a long, trackless finger of granite outcropping reaching down from far above, narrow but negotiable. Jaime actually turned toward it before he checked himself. Sure, no sign of passage would be left on the smooth stone until they quit it again, but it would be harder going for the horses and any man with Espada would know they had only to parallel it and pick up their quarry's tracks again at the upper end, so pursuit would not be slowed in the least.

Jaime realized then that he was getting strung tighter than a fiddle-gut and he fought to slacken off. He swung abruptly down and signaled Hugo to do likewise, intending to walk the blowing horses until they cooled a little, saving them against later need. Hugo shook his head.

"One or the other," the black man protested. "Not both of us afoot. One of these horses is supposed to be ridden by a woman. Your boots or mine make that kind of a print?"

Jaime swore at himself and waved Hugo on, leading the mare with Helga up, half dragging her along by main force to keep up with the horse ahead. After half a dozen yards, Helga spoke quietly.

"Give me the reins before you pull the bit out of her mouth," she said. "They haven't caught up with us yet. We'll do what we have to when they do, Jaime. The best we can manage will have to do until then."

He angrily snapped the leathers up to her and trotted ahead, wanting to run out the pressure in him. Even if he lost his guts, a man kept his head. But when he needed it most, he was losing his.

Breathing hard, in a few minutes he gained a few hundred yards on the laboring horses. Suddenly a vista opened before him and the blue lake of the *Taoseños* lay just below, close at hand. There was a small knoll here, and he scrambled up it to look back over the trees the way they had come.

For a long, anxious moment, Jaime could see no sign of pursuit, further shaking his confidence in his own judgment and intent. Then a flash of a light off to the west winked from bare metal and he glimpsed a portion of Espada's file crossing a brief opening in the timber there.

They were riding briskly but without their first eagerness when they turned off of the trade road. And they were now far wide of the fugitive tracks they should have been following up along the outcropped finger of granite.

Continuing to search intently, he presently saw that the reason for this detour was the same as before. A thin, shifting line of *Taoseños* only momentarily visible as they slipped from one cover to another, was intermittently exposed between his viewpoint and the distant file. Espada was again being forced to swing wide to avoid direct confrontation with the Indians whose intent he could not know and whose actual numbers he could not estimate.

Grateful as he had been when the Indians turned Espada back on the trade road, reestablishing the relationship of pursued and pursuit, Jaime was displeased now. However much the Comanche breed might want to recapture the woman who had tricked him into an almost disastrous situation and to settle with Hugo for his desertion and treachery, too much of this kind of unappraisable pressure might make him abandon his resumed pursuit and drive for his ultimate target on the Corona.

Wheeling, Jaime scrambled hastily back down the knoll. At its foot he found Helga and Hugo on motionless horses, uneasily facing the thin, austere figure of the ancient *cacique* of Taos. The implacable *viejo* who had called him a liar and ordered him to leave his country at once. And behind him lay the forbidden waters of the sacred blue lake of his people.

# CHAPTER 17

Jaime knew that alien presence in this holy reserve was probably the gravest affront which could be offered this old man and those he led along the paths of righteousness and law. He was certain that no justification for the intrusion would be acceptable, but there had to be some effort at explanation and defense and he started to speak. The old man held up his hand.

"A few words," he said in the voice which seemed to have the creak of his aged bones. "Listen. The day changes. Sometimes it is night. Then day again. So man changes. A people. And the law. You understand?"

Jaime shook his head. He whom Father Frederico had said knew all things waved the upraised hand impatiently.

"You understood before and much good has come from it," he continued. "Some enemies are dead, and not by Indian hands. No soldiers will come to the pueblo because of it. Those others over there must die, too?"

"The gods willing," Jaime agreed. "Before others do. Before they can cross the mountains."

"That will bring peace, an end to all of this, with no blame to us?"

"*Espero que sí*. With the right kind of luck."

"They are many," the old man said thoughtfully. "Still, it may be so. You ate the forbidden *peyotl* and had the dreams and found the place where they were. You were alone, yet you still live."

The *cacique* indicated Helga.

"There was in fact this woman. You found her, also. And this black man to help you. Now you go toward your own country. So you did not lie about that, either. You wish those others to follow you?"

Jaime nodded.

"But not too close," he added, "until we can find the right place. Most of all, I don't want them to turn back because they've lost us."

"We will not fight," the old man warned. "You know that. We will spill no more blood. But they will not turn back. I can promise you that. As long as they are on our land, they will follow you. And as you say, not too close."

He turned and leveled an arm, mere bone in leather, off to the southeast beyond the far rim of the blue lake, toward a granite crag which stood apart from higher peaks against the skyline.

"Go there. Before you reach where that mountain stands, you will come to a road you have traveled before. A little-used trail of the Utes. You will know the way from there."

"I remember."

"They will follow to that place, as you wish. Beyond, we can do nothing. It is not our country. Now, go. See nothing here as you pass. Remember nothing. We will forget, also. But tell your *yanqui ranchero grande* that at Taos we do what we can for peace, too."

"He'll be pleased," Jaime said. "They will be at Santa Fe, also. Believe me."

Tight-stretched lips long unaccustomed to a smile parted.

"It is time," the old man said. "They have long memories down there."

He started to turn away, then checked, his smile widening.

"I think your fathers slept some time in a tipi."

Jaime blinked, not understanding.

"You are too good a hunter for a *yanqui*," the *cacique* of Taos explained. "You know too many good tricks. You understand too much. You are three, but those others over there think you are two. The woman and a black man. They do not even know you exist. It will cost them when the time comes for them to learn the truth. That is Indian, my friend."

Now actually chuckling, the old man walked erectly into the timber. He disappeared almost at once, as though disembodied, but the marks of his passage flowed before him. It was Jaime's turn to smile. The wily ancient had not met them alone. God only knew how many bow-armed *Taoseños* were there, waiting for whatever signal. Now the test was past.

"Light down," he told Helga and Hugo. "We can afford to leave three tracks behind us here. Nobody else will see them. We'll walk a spell and breathe the horses."

They went along the shore of the blue lake. Aside from a small, hard-packed dance ground set back in a grove of trees, there was nothing about to indicate the nature of this place. There was no camp, no sign of human presence—indeed that humans had ever been here. If ceremonial fires were sometimes built, all trace of residue had been erased. There were no stumps or ax marks, no trodden paths and flattened brush. Only timeless peace and serenity.

Even nature had been kind. Nowhere in sight in any direction were there any of the blackened, re-growing pock marks of old lightning burns common to the timbered slopes of these mountains. It was the kind of holy place which Jaime found he could understand. It was not hard to believe that gods were indeed close to such a place.

The little bowl cradling the lake fell away as they climbed the gentle slope of the south rim. Remounting here, they followed a sidehill around at the same level to the next ridge and climbed over this. Dropping down the far side, they cut the old, slow, meandering buffalo trail through the mountains to the headwaters of the Cimarroncito. Both Helga and Hugo recognized it at once and Jaime could see at a distance the little canyon of the stream he had followed down from the western slope of El Cumbre Pass.

Leaving his companions to rest the horses again, Jaime climbed back up the slope they had just descended until he had a satisfactory view back down the trail toward the Taos plateau. It was several minutes before Espada's file of men, eleven riders in single file, appeared. They were descending the same ridge on which he stood, perhaps a mile to the west.

When they reached the trail at the foot of the ridge, they turned along it toward him without hesitation. He watched carefully a few moments for some sign of escorting or flanking Indians but could detect none. At least the *cacique* had kept his promise. Espada was following, and shortly he would again have the incentive of fresh tracks.

Jaime returned to the trail, taking care to come the last few feet along the trunk of a big deadfall tree, the butt of which jutted over a large rock beside the trail. Helga and Hugo rode to him and he stepped from the rock to the back of the mare behind the girl.

When they turned from the Ute trail onto the lesser game track accompanying the stream he had followed down from the distant base of El Cumbre, Jaime took special pains to be sure signs that they had turned up were plain without being too obvious. They rode faster, then, not wanting their lead over Espada cut down too much.

Jaime counted the time carefully, making the best estimate he could, and when he thought Espada's party would be close enough to the junction of the tracks, he pulled up, drawing his belt-gun.

"They won't know anything about El Cumbre," he said. "They won't know where we're headed—may think we're lost, in fact. But they do know the Ute trail and where it goes. They may decide to give you two up and take it direct for the Corona. If so, I'm going to give them a reason to change their minds. I'm going to let them know just how close we are."

He raised the gun to fire a shot in the air. Hugo leaned quickly from saddle to catch his arm.

"Wait! Don't waste powder. They're sure to wonder why a shot. Suspect it, even. But they won't this. Best off, they'll know it's me. They've heard it often enough. And we can keep moving to make it real. Like me and Missy didn't know they're within a thousand miles."

The black man leaned back in his saddle and opened his mouth. His deep voice boomed out with astonishing volume and clarity in a rollicking bawdy song about a big-balled boll weevil and what he did to a planter's cotton and his woman besides because Master tried to keep a good man down.

At the chorus, Hugo kicked his horse up. The mare moved of her own accord, and they rode on up the stream at a pace Jaime hoped equaled that of those behind them. As the exploits of the big, black boll weevil became more lurid and spectacular, Helga Cagle began to laugh for the first time since they had escaped from Turley's. And on the next chorus, she joined Hugo's rolling bass in a strong, harmonious contralto counterpoint, the words monosyllabic but the melody true.

When the chorus was finished, Hugo was vastly admiring.

"Where'd a pretty little lady like you learn a dirty old song like that?" he demanded.

"Down in the Missouri bottoms, he was a traveling preacher-man," Helga said. "Passing out the gospel, according to his lights. Same tune, and he did it the same way your old boll weevil got his revenge, only with maybe a little bit more imagination."

The black man's grin widened.

"Missy, the way I learned that song, it don't take hardly any imagination at all—"

He was interrupted by the sharp, whip-like crack which distinguished the report of a well-charged rifle from the deeper, slightly more sustained sound of a hand-gun. Hugo turned his grin to Jaime.

"See? It worked."

Jaime nodded. Despite echo characteristics in such broken terrain, the direction and general location of the source of the sound were unmistakable.

"They've turned off the buffalo trail after us. We've got them, now."

"More'n that," Hugo said. "They think they've got us. I been waiting for that shot. For the pot. Bound to be getting hungry, now. Or going to be. Knocked themselves over a muley ear or a white-tail. Wouldn't do it unless they was sure the missy and me couldn't double back past 'em or something. So they'll be stopping directly to roast up some meat."

"A couple of them, maybe," Jamie corrected. "Not all, if they've got any sense. They can eat later, when the cooked meat's caught up with them again."

He pointed ahead, up past the timberline toward which they were steadily climbing. The great peaks among which the tortuous passage of El Cumbre lay were separating themselves from lesser mountains, aligning themselves in a seemingly impassable barrier.

"Even if they still think it's only you and Helga they're tracking, they'll know better than to let you get up there in that rock ahead of them, where trailing's a hell of a lot harder and you could hole up anywhere. Most of them'll come on hard, now we've let them know just where we are. Time to hump, and hump like hell."

"Then let's go," Hugo said urgently, accepting Jaime's reasoning without question. "I sure as hell don't want supper with them!"

They rode as rapidly as possible up the course of the little stream they had been following until the horses began to blow again. Leaving choice of trail to Hugo, who was in the lead, Jaime rode behind Helga on the mare, twisting frequently to watch behind. It was important, now, to find not only the easiest way for the horses but also one which would not expose them to a view from below. When necessary, he called a change ahead to Hugo in order to avoid this.

Presently, in a little streamside park through which they had passed less than half an hour before, a thin line of blue smoke spiraled into the air and Jamie realized Hugo had been right: at least a part of Espada's force had stopped to roast their kill. These men would be delayed by the cooking process, which even with the quick, hot fire of deadfall aspen, would take as much as three hours with the lower boiling temperature of juices at this altitude. Jaime remembered how long it had taken coffee to boil on his solitary descent of El Cumbre.

But he was also certain that he had been right, too, and that the Comanche breed, with his quarry so close, would come on with the rest of his men, hoping to overtake the fugitives and deal with them before shadows lengthened further and light failed. However, by taking advantage of convolutions in the ascending course of the creek, which kept the lower terrain obscured, they managed to reach the place where Jaime had struck the creek on his descent. Here they turned from the stream toward the base of the pass itself.

The way steepened as they climbed from the little canyon and for the first time Jaime risked dismounting all three of them to save the horses. Knowing the way, he took the lead. Helga followed, leading the mare, then Hugo and his horse. Jaime hoped his own tracks would be obscured enough by those following to make it unlikely for any to read the passage of three instead of two, particularly so since Espada and his men had no reason to suspect Hugo and Helga were not alone.

It was hard, grueling work with only the consolation that this steep a pitch would be no easier for those behind. Across the canyon, reaching shadows blended together as the sun sank lower, smudging off toward dark, but on this western slope, warm red light lingered interminably, as though to deliberately illuminate them for those behind. And as they approached the harsh bleakness of timberline, separated from the rocky haven of broken granite and great boulders marking the actual foot of El Cumbre itself by a broad, open tundra-belt of alpine bunch-grass, Jaime felt tension winding tight in him again.

He detoured a little to stay with the last tongue of squat, twisted, storm-scarred trees until they petered out altogether, then called a halt beside the little stone cairn which marked the faint trail up from Santa Fe to the pass. Halting here, breathing painfully in the increasingly thin air, he studied the way back toward the creek from which they had ascended. He could detect no movement, but was not reassured. There was ample cover there.

Moving fifty yards or so away from his companions and the blowing horses, Jaime steadied the sound of his own breathing as much as possible, held his breath, faced into the gentle upslope wind, and turned his ears slowly from side to side. In the silence of this high place, the light breeze was a roar against his eardrums, and although his breath was stayed, he could hear the rhythmic, liquid surge of his heart and the coursing of blood through his head.

He inhaled deeply a few times, checked, and listened again. On the third try, the message came, the solid ring of an iron shoe on rock, the flatulent, protesting grunt of a fast-climbing horse, the roll of a loose stone, other small sounds of movement without identity, all spelling out more than one rider. Several more. Soft sounds, indistinguishable elsewhere, but clearly riding this high silence. Distant, still, but too close. Much too close.

Jaime spun and looked up across the stretch of open bunch-grass tundra to the nearest talus slope of broken rock spilled down from the great peaks flanking the notch over which El Cumbre climbed. They had almost made it. Almost, but not quite. He sprinted back to his companions, running awkwardly and with tantalizing slowness, as though some elastic string was restraining him.

Reaching the mare, he grabbed the two rifles and one of the extra belt-guns, pressing the other on Helga.

"Mount up, both of you," he ordered. "We can't make it across to the rocks together before they're into the clear. Get all you can out of the horses. I'll cover you from here. When you're set, you can cover me."

Hugo nodded and swung up at once, clearing his own gun for use. Helga started to protest. Jaime thrust her against the horse.

"Now, God damn it!"

He cupped his hands and she stepped into them. He slapped the mare's rump before Helga was down in the seat and Hugo rode after her.

The stout, stubborn taproot of one of the gnarled old trees had snapped in some winter gale and its lesser roots had pulled up a big disk of sod and stone as it went over. Jaime dived behind this, put his extra guns carefully at hand, and briefly watched Helga and the black man.

They rode as he had run afoot, with agonizing slowness for all the effort of the winded horses. The way he remembered movement in boyhood nightmares when he dreamed he was trying to escape some nameless terror. And the distance to the huge, tumbled rock heaps of the talus slope seemed interminable, although he knew it could not be more than a few hundred yards.

He twisted back around, thrust his own rifle out

over the dwarfed trunk of the blasted old tree, and
waited, breathing as deeply and steadily as he could
so that the sights would also steady when he needed
them.

The wait was even more brief than he had feared it
would be. He could not afford to look again, but he
thought that Helga and Hugo could be no more than
half across to the talus slope when Espada and his
men broke from thinning cover below. They rode
scarcely faster than their mounted quarry and on
equally winded horses, but there were nine of them.
Only two, then, had been left behind to cook their kill
and bring the meat on.

And they had already seen Helga and Hugo, for
they were fanned out abreast instead of in file, so that
each had a clear line of fire up at their fleeing targets,
and they had changed course a little to ride straight
for them.

Jaime's cheek snugged to the stock of his rifle. He
had been at great pains to keep his presence secret
from them. Now was the time to reveal it.

# CHAPTER 18

Spread out as they were, at intervals of a dozen yards or so, Espada and his men made difficult targets. And Espada, himself, was at the outermost wing and therefore the most distant.

Jaime waited a slow count, gauging their progress against what ground he thought he could cover behind him when they flushed him out. He realized he was not going to be able to let them closer than maximum rifle range without risking being ridden down and shot from behind when he broke from cover in retreat. Much as he wanted to take out the leader first, if possible, Espada's greater distance forced him to choose another target.

He sighted on the other Indian in the party, believing him more important than any of the Yankees if there was stalking to be done later. Correcting for the natural tendency to overshoot on a downhill shot because of lengthened carry, he set the bead of the front sight a handbreadth above the horn of the man's saddle. As the horse reached into its next stride, straining head down and clear of the line of fire, he eased off the shot.

The bullet struck the Indian somewhere near the belt. He was torn from his saddle, arms asprawl and one leg flung high by the violence of the shock. The other foot, despite the smooth flexibility of its moccasin, went through its stirrup and hung up as the man spilled off that side, headfirst to the ground. He dangled there by the imprisoned foot, head and shoulders dragging as the frightened horse danced sidewise away.

The surprise was total, the bullet arriving even ahead of the sound of the shot. To take advantage of the consternation while he could, Jaime snatched up the other rifle, sighted swiftly, and squeezed the trigger. There was a sickening snap as the weapon misfired. And there was no time to scrabble for another cap and reprime the charge. Espada had sighted the smoke-ball of the shot and was yelling at his men, urging them forward.

Belting the extra hand-gun and grabbing the now useless rifles, Jaime leaped to his feet and ran upslope across the open, bunch-grassed tundra. The footing was uneven, the tufts of grass surprisingly slippery under the hard soles of his boots. Ahead, urging their horses to the utmost, Helga and Hugo were still yards short of the nearest rocks. Behind, guns opened up.

Glancing back, Jaime saw that they were being fired from the saddle, a useless exercise at this distance. But the horsemen were cutting that down fast. Jaime slipped, tripped, and fell heavily. Scrambling up, he saw that Hugo had seen the spill and misunderstood, thinking him hit by the gunfire behind. The black man started to saw his horse around. Jaime waved him on, urgently.

Helga reached the rocks and disappeared among them. A moment later gunsmoke blossomed there and he heard the pistol-ball pass over his head. Another wasted shot, but it had the desired effect, drawing another volley from Espada's force, further emptying the charged cylinders they had available. Hugo reached the rocks and vanished among them.

Jaime glanced behind him again. Pursuit had cut the distance in half and he saw Espada signal the thing he feared most, caught in the open as he was. Two riflemen pulled up sharply at the signal, both kneeling for a steady shot. Legs pistoning and lungs sobbing at the thin air, he drove on because there was nothing else he could do.

The shots came almost together. One sang spitefully away from stone in the bunchgrass, within inches of his boot. The second, like a vengeful echo, burned across the inside of his left elbow and down across the hard muscle of his forearm to strike the extra rifle a hammer blow just ahead of his gripping fingers.

The weapon was smashed from his numbed grip and spun to the tundra. He grabbed for it, but his shock-cramped fingers would not respond. Pistols opened up behind again and he was forced to abandon the weapon. He fell again, scrambled up without being able to use his left arm, and ran on. In the rocks ahead and above him, a pistol fired twice with deliberation. A horse screamed, downslope, and he heard it go down, heavily.

There were more shots, above and below. Stone dust stung his face and he was among the rocks, great tumbled blocks as big as the main house on the Corona. In an overhang among them, sheltered from below and above as well, stood the two heaving horses. A little aside, crouched at a small aperture which commanded the slope below, were Helga and the black man, now holding their fire as Jaime staggered up to them.

Helga blanched at the slow drip of blood from the sleevecuff of his bullet-burned arm. Jaime thrust her back and turned up the cuff to reassure her. The nearly spent ball had burred up the skin over the protruding crazy-bone on the inside of his elbow and plowed a shallow furrow down his forearm before smashing the misfired rifle from his hand. The numbed and drawn-up fingers of his left hand slackened and feeling began to return with a few flexings of his elbow. She eased, then, and let him be.

Espada, knowing the folly of charging on into an enemy securely holed up in such granite cover, had turned his men back moments before Jaime dodged into the shelter of the rocks. One of them had reclaimed the abandoned misfired rifle and was waving it triumphantly over his head.

They left behind them a dead horse. Its rider ran stumblingly at another's stirrup as they hastily dropped back downslope to where the dead man's horse still nervously shied from the bloody thing dangling from a stirrup and dragging unprotestingly across the tufted tundra.

The dismounted man ran to the shying horse, freed the body, and mounted up, quieting the animal with his weight and authority. Those who had discharged their weapons began reloading. They did so hastily, without taking time to swab out the bores before measuring fresh charges. By this Jaime judged Espada intended to close again at once if he could.

Jaime glanced at the flattening angle of the fire-ball sun over the distant mountains beyond the canyon of the Rio Grande. Shadows were dark and it was already nearly night in the lowland deeps along the river. Light would last longer here on the high peaks. But it would go with startling swiftness when the sun went.

"Good for another climb before dark?" he asked.

Hugo was recharging the pistol chambers he and Helga had fired. Both of them nodded. Jaime smiled.

"They think they've got us holed here. And Espada will want to wait for the two they left at the fire below to catch up. He'll likely try to send some around to get above us while the rest keep us pinned down. I want a better place than this to spend the night."

"Suits me," Helga answered. "If it's got a bed and a hot bath."

"All the comforts of home," Jaime promised.

He nodded for them to bring the horses on lead and led off through the great, fragmented boulders, finding crevices through which the animals could pass without revealing their movement below.

Jaime kept them among the rocks, threading tortuously through them, trading the easy going for constant cover. They seemed to climb no faster than the line between light and dark now rising out of the depths behind them. Finally the climb leveled. A little stream trickled down from ice fields above and across a small pocket of sand imprisoned by overhanging crags and almost completely sheltered from the night wind Jaime knew would come. Ahead, the immediate way seemed downgrade. Jaime pulled up here. Helga breathed a sigh of relief as she slid stiffly down from the mare.

"Thank God!" she said. "Now I know how this pass got its reputation. I thought we'd never make the top."

Jaime smiled. Leaving Hugo to unsaddle and get their gear down and water the horses, he gestured for Helga to follow. Finding a suitable chimney, they climbed up out of the pocket far enough to bring the sky-piercing ultimate summits of the mountains into view. The backbone of the Sangre de Cristos was much closer, now. In fact, their viewpoint was far up on the shoulder of the divide.

Jaime pointed to the notch of a saddle between two of the highest peaks, the tips of which were now pink with the last of the sun, already gone below the western horizon.

"That's El Cumbre," he told Helga. "Over that and we're home. Practically."

Helga stared upward with disbelief.

"Practically! There's a practical way over that?"

"It can be done."

"When?"

"Tomorrow. If we don't have too much company left. Maybe the next day."

"How far?"

Jaime shrugged.

"Miles? I don't know. You got to count the up and down, too. Three-four hours, if we had our wind and fresh horses and nothing else on our minds. Them, for instance—"

He turned her and pointed back down the way they had come. About a mile above the foot of the rock-field, where they had hit cover and made their first stand against him, Espada and three of his men were coming down from a higher side-slope, to which they had circled, into the massive labyrinth of tumbled stone choking the bottom of the steeply slanting draw. They were angling back, now, toward their companions left below. Presently they disappeared into a fissure which hid their further descent from view.

Helga sucked a deep breath.

"I see now why you wanted to get higher before we stopped. They'd have us trapped if we'd stayed where we were."

She turned and looked up the col they had been ascending. It was a forbidding barrier, but she straightened with determined effort.

"Why don't we do it right, then, Jaime?" she asked. "Keep on going. All night, if we have to. Over the top, up there. They couldn't possibly overtake us with a lead like that, even if we do have to ride one horse double when we can mount up again. No way for them to get to the ranch ahead of us, then."

Jaime shook his head.

"And have it all to do in the ranch yard, sooner or later?" he protested. "Better up here. I started out to do a job and I'm going to finish it. All of it. If any of us cross that notch up there, it's going to be an easy ride home. We'll damned well know there's nobody behind us."

"That isn't all, is it?" she probed, eyeing him soberly. "It's partly because of me. Because I'm a woman."

"Well, now you mention it, yes," Jaime agreed. "I started out to bring back a pretty damned something hunk of woman, all smooth and soft and feisty. More, if I've reckoned her right. And I aim to find out, directly."

"Not here, you don't."

"I didn't say. Next pick of time and place is mine. You had yours, and then got buck fever. But I sure as hell ain't going to haul you back all gaunted up and wind-broke and saddle-sored and rock-burned, either. Spence Stanton would kick my ass clean to Missouri for treating first-class stock that way."

Helga made a rude noise with her lips and smiled at him wearily.

"Bullshit," she said quietly. "No use trying to sweet-talk me that way. You think I can't make it without a rest."

"More'n that. I know you can't. Or Hugo or me, either. Not at night. I did it once. That's enough. No man's got that much luck twice, and I figure I'm fresh out. We'll have first light. We'll tackle her then."

They worked back down the chimney into the pocket where they had left Hugo with the horses and gear. The horses were there, but there was no sign of the black man in the rapidly failing light. Then there was a whisper of sound and he materialized behind them. He indicated the crevice from which he had stepped. He had spread their blankets on the clean sand within.

"Your room, Missy," he said. "Sorry about the hot bath."

Helga bent to investigate and the lowering night suddenly came alive with sound. It started with one shot, overlapped by a ragged volley of others. Such were the angles and planes of the vast slabs and pinnacles of bare, living stone towering about them that echoes leaped from every surface, diminishing in volume only as they bounded away into a great distance in the night.

The effect was of a sudden outburst of full-scale warfare about them; below, above, on every side, seeming at point-blank range, climaxed by an angry yelling which also engulfed them before it, too, ricocheted off into the empty silence of distance. Startled, Hugo and Helga looked anxiously to Jaime. He sat down on the sand and leaned against a vertical slant of rock.

"Jumpy, down there," he said with satisfaction. "And too dark, now, to see good. Espada and them with him come onto the rest sooner than they expected. Must have figured they were us. Or the other way around. Be kind of interesting to count noses in the morning."

"They sounded terribly close," Helga said, instinctively whispering.

Jaime shook his head.

"Night does that to sound up here for some reason. Just got to remember it works both ways. They're down at the foot of the rocks. They'll stay put till it's light again. They'll have to."

# CHAPTER 19

There was no further sound from below. The horses moved restlessly to complain the lack of forage, but settled presently in proof of weariness from the long climb. Hugo broke out some more of his cured meat and they munched it in the awesomely silent darkness, finding it somehow not as palatable as before.

Hugo grunted softly.

"Sure could do with a fire and some hot pone to go with this."

"And one of 'Mana's currant pies," Helga agreed. "Your hotel don't set the best table ever, Jaime."

"Hell, this is high on the hog, woman. You ought to try it alone up here sometime. That's when it really gets to you. And the wind, when you're in the open. We'll make out fine."

The stars lowered, becoming increasingly brilliant where they were not blacked out by the bulk of the mountains: the two dippers, the blazing belt from which hung Orion's sword, and the broad running-W which Spence Stanton said was Cassiopeia, the Rocking Chair, swinging imperceptibly around to mark the slow passage of time. Familiar beacons and old friends, seemingly almost within reach in the crystalline air.

Helga tired in a little while and offered to share the blankets again. Jaime and Hugo both refused for the same reason, though neither voiced it. Both knew there was not room on this mountain for the man who called himself Espada and sleep. Not tonight.

Soon after Helga turned in under the sand-floored crevice Hugo had smoothed for her, there was a distant, thin, high snap like that of bursting sap in a winter-frozen pine. It was high above them on the scarp of one of the mother peaks. It was followed by a whole orchestration of numbing sound as the first little stress-ridden rocks slid and tumbled and bounded down the mountain in the hurtling stone anvils of a full-scale rock fall.

If the mountain itself did not shake, the air did, and the reverberations thundered on for what seemed minutes before muttering off into silence. When the last echoes were gone, Hugo, invisible in the darkness, drew an awed breath.

"David," the black man murmured. And when Jaime made no response, "With a stone he slew Goliath. The works of the Lord are mighty."

"Amen," Jaime agreed, practically depleting his Scriptural familiarity in a word.

Hugo remained silent thereafter and Jaime sat long, going carefully over the climb ahead as he remembered it from his previous crossing of El Cumbre. He was not so sure of God, but the odds were long and if a man knew the land well enough, maybe both could be made to work for him. They would need that.

The sun came explosively, for it had already long been high above the plains to the east when it surmounted the curtain of peaks flanking the pass. It came down hot and hard, glancing dazzlingly from the myriad crystalline flecks in the gray granite walls surrounding them and almost instantly dissipating remnant night chill.

While Hugo and the girl saddled, Jaime climbed the little chimney he had used before. Espada and his men were already on the move. As he feared they might with the return of light, they were abandoning fallen rock choking the floor of the col for the less tortuous if more exposed going of the sidewall above the talus slope, making the climb no less arduous but considerably faster.

It was plain at once that if Jaime and his companions kept to their previous course and cover among the rocks, they would be overtaken before they reached the summit, with all loss of advantage and the enemy between them and their objective on the Corona. He carefully counted the file behind the Comanche breed and smiled a little to himself, remembering the gunsound which had reverberated up from below when Espada and those in advance with him had turned back to the position of the others at first dark. He dropped quickly back down the chimney.

Jaime again took his rifle and one of the extra handguns, passing the other as before to Helga.

"They're trying to bypass us," he reported to his companions. "They'll make it, too, if we don't do something to slow them up. One good thing, though. They're one short this morning."

"Those shots last night?" Hugo asked.

"One of the dangers on a hunt of coming back to even a friendly camp after dark," Jaime agreed. " 'Shoot first and ask questions afterward' can nail a friend as easy as an enemy. So there's nine, now."

"Got to do better than that before we top the pass," the black man said.

Jaime nodded.

"Aim to, and I want no argument, this time, from either of you. Start working up out of these rocks to the top of the fall on this side. What trail there is runs there. Watch close and you can keep to it by some little rock cairns like I showed you below.

"They're working up along the other side and still quite a ways below, so you'll be out of range when you come into the open. With luck, they'll still believe there's only you two. They won't be expecting me. I'll work on up through the rocks, keeping to cover, and see if I can't give 'em reason to wonder some. Slow 'em up anyway."

"No, Jaime," Helga said flatly. "I told you before. We stick together. Isn't there someplace we can ambush them?"

"I've got one in mind, up yonder a ways, but I want you two and the horses past it before I try it. Don't worry. I'll be in cover. Even in the rocks I can make faster time than you and Hugo can with the horses. I'll catch up before you're to the top. Don't forget, I've been over this before. Now, get going. We're losing too much time."

Helga looked to the black man in appeal. Hugo shrugged.

"I'm fresh out of better ideas, Missy," he said.

He swung up and rode into the next crevice above. Helga hesitated.

"God damn it—" Jaime began.

"All right, you stubborn son of a bitch," Helga said. "But if you get yourself killed again, I'll never forgive you."

"*Como siempre,*" Jaime agreed.

He cupped his hands. She stepped up onto the Corona mare and rode after Hugo without looking back. Jaime took another crevice at a slightly divergent angle, moving swiftly. He climbed steadily for a good fifteen minutes, then found a vantage which afforded him cover. He could see the south slope along which Espada and his men had been working.

They were closer than he expected, and as he watched, they pulled up momentarily in reaction to something beyond him across the col on the north slope where the marked trail over El Cumbre lay. He shifted position and saw that Hugo and Helga had come out of the rocks at the top of the broken talus slope into the open. He saw with relief that Hugo had found a cairn, and they were on the trail. But it was a steep pitch there and they were forced to dismount and lead the horses, slowing them more than he liked.

Espada saw their labored climbing and took instant advantage of it, gambling the freshness of his horses

against an immediate end to the long pursuit. They
came down to the head of the talus slope and disappeared intermittently there among the rocks, coming
on fast and as direct as passages among the great
boulders would allow, almost straight at Jaime's position.

He had not counted on this. He had thought they
would stay on their own side of the col and that he
could work along parallel, flanking them as they came
up, and pick single targets. Now he would have to
deal with the lot at once, snap-shooting at best if he
was not to be flushed out and overrun, himself. And
the delay he might cause would be proportionately
less.

Jaime ran a few yards up the floor of the col, darting
among massively heaped boulders, to get a little above
the line of passage of Espada's party if he could.
When the sounds of their approach were as close as he
dared risk, he scrambled up a chimney between great
rocks to the summit of one, sprawling out flat there.

A glance across told him that Helga and Hugo were
still laboring up the steep pitch they had encountered
on the trail on the far side, apparently unaware of or
unable to see Espada's change of course toward them.
Then Espada, himself, flashed across a narrow opening between huge boulders. Jaime snugged his cheek
against the stock of his rifle and counted those following the Comanche, waiting for the ninth man.

As a boy, he had taken geese in this way with his
old unrifled squirrel gun, trying to pick off the last of a
flight coming in to water. If he had luck, those ahead
did not seem aware of what was happening behind
them and did not spook off, even at the sound of gunfire. He had heard that in the old days, Indians foot-
hunting buffalo had loosed their arrows in the same
way, picking off the last animal in a file first without
alarming the rest.

Allowing a fair lead behind the eighth man, he
squeezed off his shot as the head of the ninth man's

horse appeared in the slot. Man and bullet met. The rider stood spasmodically in his stirrups, tilted off to one side, and smashed headfirst into a wall of stone as the horse passed close against one of the great boulders.

*Eight* . . .

Keeping his head down, rasping boots and pants and burning hide, Jamie slid thirty feet down the steep side of the rock to its base. He crouched an instant there, listening, then swore softly to himself. The riders had halted abruptly at the sound of his shot. In the utter silence, he could not pinpoint their exact location.

That was, he knew, the Indian in Espada. Ears were no less valuable to a hunter than his eyes. Seizing a half-pound chunk of stone, Jaime flung it as far as he could back among the rocks the way he had come. It made an astonishing clatter as it landed. He flung another off at right angles and was sprinting and dodging on up through the boulders before it landed with another loud clattering.

There was a yell of imprecation and horses were instantly in motion again, splitting into two groups, he thought. He held to his sprint, making as little noise as possible, for a hundred yards or so until he reached a deep, slotted passage too narrow for a mounted man. He crouched in the entrance to this and started to recharge his rifle.

Before he could set the ball and recap the long gun, a man briefly appeared beyond range of his pistols. Then another burst from between rocks, almost at point-blank range, coming straight toward him. Encumbered as he was by the rifle, he was rushed in clearing his pistol and missed his first shot. The man saw him and reined desperately aside, firing his gun as he did so. Powdered stone stung Jaime's cheek as he shot the man cleanly from saddle.

Darting out, he caught the reins of the rearing

horse, vaulted up, and spurred it into a wider passage up the col. The man who had appeared out of range reappeared behind him and shouted alarm to the others. Bending low, Jaime raked his spurs with grim satisfaction.

*Seven . . .*

And now he was mounted, with his enemies behind him again.

Helga halted, almost blocking the trail, rooted in alarm at the sudden volley of shots which had broken out below—one, followed by two more, almost on top of each other. An exchange, not a single sniping shot such as the first few moments before had been. So at least some of Espada's men had closed with Jaime.

She and Hugo were almost at the head of the steep pitch they had been laboring up afoot. A great, hanging cliff stood sheer above the trail here and the echoes of the shots banged thunderously against it, multiplying them to infinity. She tried to find the source of the shots below, some trace of Jaime for reassurance. But Hugo was angrily, frantically shouldering past her horse, dragging his own, thrusting roughly at her, yelling something, forcing her into an awkward, hasty scramble on up the trail. Something in his urgency made her obey, although she kept trying to look below as she half-ran to keep up with his insistence.

Then the angle of his blanched, upturned face made her lift her eyes. Far up the face of the cliff towering above them, falling with deceptive laziness, was a clot of loosened rock as big as a wagon. Badly winded by the long, hard climb behind them, she would not have thought she could do better than she already was, but suddenly she had new strength and was dragging at her horse as Hugo was his.

She heard a whistling sound. There was a scattering of pebbles, the smell of dust. The whistling became a roar and the earth underfoot shook as the rock fall landed. Hugo stopped and leaned limply against his horse, his eyes closed. She turned her head.

Imbedded in the trail, itself, where she had first stopped, a scant few yards below them, lay a great chunk of stone and a heap of lesser ones which still seemed to be settling. She stared with rounded eyes, awed at the narrow margin by which death had passed. She heard Hugo's voice.

"Thank God, Missy."

She shuddered, looked at him, and nodded woodenly. He took the lead of both horses and resumed slowly up the slope. She followed uncertainly on legs which trembled beneath her.

In a few moments, they reached the top of the pitch and halted briefly to blow the horses. Helga sank wearily to the ground and looked anxiously below. It was Hugo who spotted them, drawing her attention. A file of familiar, hated riders, led by Espada, working up through the rocks toward the trail and the foot of the steep pitch they had just climbed.

She counted them automatically as they appeared: Josiah, McBain, the others, one by one, until there were seven. No more followed. So there had been a confrontation, and Jaime had not stopped the first bullet in the fusillade whose echoes had loosened the rock fall. He had emptied saddles. But he had not reappeared, himself. Foreboding shook her. He too had been shot in the exchange.

Then she saw him, mounted now on a captured horse, still ahead of Espada's group, but with hardly more than a gunshot lead. He emerged from tumbled rocks onto the trail at the foot of the steep pitch they had just topped. He was urging his mount to its best. But when he reached the pitch he had to dismount as they had done, hurrying on afoot with the animal on lead.

At this point he must have become visible to those below as well, for a man loosed a shot before Espada's angry gesture put an end to powder wastage at such range. Jaime looked back, then Helga saw the upturn of his face as he spotted her above, watching his ascent and the stubborn pursuit behind him.

He waved urgently at them and Helga scrambled to her feet, realizing he was signaling them to resume on toward the ultimate summit of the pass, now barely half a mile above. They remounted and rode on, a turn of the trail almost immediately obscuring their view of Jaime and his pursuit.

# CHAPTER 20

With Helga and her black companion again in motion above him, Jaime was relieved. He could now focus his whole attention on the men behind and the delicate, dangerous task of timing which lay ahead. The slightest miscalculation and his plan would fail. Hugo and the girl would be on their own, then, with a far shorter lead than he would have liked. There could be no mistake.

As he labored up the steep pitch afoot, his commandeered horse protesting and reluctant on lead, he could plainly hear the horses of Espada and his remaining men, pressing to overtake him. Slowed as he was, they were succeeding. Not too fast, he prayed, not too goddamned fast.

He did not look behind but kept his eyes on the great, sheer curtain of stone soaring over the steep, narrow trail ahead. Helga and the black man had disappeared behind a convolution further on and he knew they would shortly be approaching the summit of El Cumbre.

The sun was hot and he began to sweat profusely, his lungs reaching hard for the thin, dry air. Presently he saw above him a great block of granite and lesser detritus blocking the narrow trail. It had not been there on his own crossing of the pass. He remembered this place well and had thought long about it last night, concluding that it suited his purpose better than any other he remembered.

Now he was not so sure, and he wondered how

Hugo and the girl had got their horses past it. But
since they had, there would be a way for him, too, if it
did not slow him too much. As he worked his way up
along its base, the great wall of rock hanging over him
seemed to grow more ominous, and he glanced upward more often with an apprehension he could not
completely subdue.

The Utes said there were gods on El Cumbre who
swallowed men and climbers who disappeared without a trace. It was a place for only the fearless and
desperate and no man was safe from one timberline to
the other. There had to be some fact in the legend,
for the Utes were not a superstitious people, and there
was often ancient wisdom preserved in such tipi tales.

He had almost reached the recent rock fall when a
shout sounded below, closer and sooner than he liked.
He looked back. Espada and the six with him had
emerged from the tumbled rocks on the floor of the col
onto the trail at the foot of the pitch he was climbing.
They had closed distance considerably. Espada
stepped down clear of his horse, knelt at a convenient
rest, and sighted his rifle.

Jaime winced as the muzzle of the weapon belched
smoke. The bullet came, spanging away harmlessly
from stone a few yards below him, and then the
sound, booming against cliffs above him. Jaime's eyes
darted instinctively upward, but the sound bounded
away to nothing and silence returned. He eased and
glanced below again. Espada remounted, electing to
tax his horses in an attempt to close the distance a little more before expending more powder.

The man knew what he was doing. Jaime knew he
would be completely exposed until he could reach the
top of the pitch, and he had to let those below close
up a little more, perhaps even quite a little, if the timing was to be right. The rest was in the hands of the
gods of El Cumbre. Nevertheless, it rasped every
nerve in his body almost uncontrollably to keep his
back to his enemies and continue his own climb.

When he reached the recent rock fall he had spotted from below, he discovered a narrow but adequate passage around the heap and it became a useful mark behind him, to which he paid increasingly frequent attention in relationship to Espada's party as he ground his way on up the slope. His one effort now was to keep far enough ahead to avoid more shots from below and still be close enough to make his own stand as he had planned when respective positions were right.

He had almost reached the top of the pitch, just a few yards below the spot where he had seen Helga and Hugo when Espada, at the head of his file, took his horse gingerly around the rubble of the rock fall. Jaime paused, as though involuntarily for breath, and watched carefully, calculating time and distance and warning. One man followed Espada past the fallen rock, then another. As the third started through the passage, Jaime dropped his reins.

Thrusting swiftly past his horse to be clear of the animal, he threw his rifle to his shoulder and fired, not sighting at the men below but at the telltale scar of recently exposed stone far up on the face of the overhanging cliff. Dropping the rifle, he emptied one of his pistols as rapidly as he could at the same target.

At the first shot, Espada's men, believing themselves under fire, opened up at the man above them. Bullets sang close and the sound of their guns, mingling with Jaime's own, sent a multiplied thunder of echoes drumming from the great cliff and the peaks above.

Hastily reloading, they did not see a huge, acre-size slab of rock loosen itself along some old seam or fault near the raw scar at which Jaime had fired. Fragmenting in midair as it fell, turning lazily, the shattered massif descended majestically and with awesome finality.

When awareness did come to the entrapped men, there was no time nor place to go. Jaime thought that Espada, fighting his panicked horse a few yards past the debris of the earlier rock fall, was clear, as he had planned. That was the important thing. About the others he could not tell, nor did it matter.

A horse screamed. So did a man, an involuntary bray of horror. Then the fragmented aerial mass cascaded onto the trail with shuddering force. Dust exploded from it, obscuring all. Dropping his empty pistol beside his discharged rifle and clutching his extra weapon in his hand, Jaime sprinted back down the trail toward the cataclysm he had created.

As he reached the settling mushroom of dust, two men reeled from it, thick-coated with powdered granite and bleeding from wounds caused by splintering debris. Neither was Espada, but rather the two men closest behind him, Jaime thought in disappointment. He believed them too dazed to be of further threat and would have let them be, but both saw him at the same time.

By some perception forged of such massive disaster, each seemed to understand he had brought this about and both savagely jerked belt weapons free. Reluctantly but with dispassionate efficiency, Jaime fired twice before they could steady themselves on their feet. Both fell and lay without movement.

A screaming commenced again and he came upon a horse in the murk, half-buried and with a broken back, senselessly trying to rise on uninjured forequarters. He shot it behind the ear and there was silence again except for a faint trickling of pebble-sized fragments somewhere. A little beyond he found another horse, Espada's he believed, standing headdown, reins trailing. It was trembling violently, its hide blooded in several places by flying stone chips and fragments but otherwise seemingly unhurt.

He went on a few steps more toward the great mound of broken stone emerging from the dust and completely blocking the trail and rising to a height of twenty feet or more. Beneath it lay the others and their mounts.

Beneath it lay Espada. Without Espada the task

he had set himself was not done and never could be.
He had rescued Helga Cagle and in a little while
would return her unharmed to the Corona. He had
kept his own oath and had his own vengeance, both
for himself and for the woman he loved. But without
Espada to identify the conspirators, he had failed in
his duty to Spence Stanton, to the Territory, and to the
iron for which he rode. In this the tracking, the bait-
ing, and the long, dangerous pursuit had failed. In this
he had failed. And in his book there could be no
failure in a man entrusted as *segundo*.

He started to turn back, to catch up his commandeered horse, retrieve his guns, and climb on to wherever Helga and their black companion might be
waiting, knowing their anxiety over the gunfire and the
outcome here, but suddenly right at his boot toes, dust-
covered rock turned over and rose, erupting as from
the earth itself, becoming a man. A tall, powerful, desperately vengeful man, hatless and wild-eyed, with the
handsome, feral features of the best of three dark
races. Espada, from the grave, itself, with a cocked
gun in his upsweeping hand.

Instinctively, wholly reflexively, Jaime struck down
and outward, hard, with the barrel of his own weapon,
striking the Comanche breed's gun-arm somewhere
near the wrist. The gun fired even as it was driven
from the man's hand but the shot went wild and Jaime
saw the weapon disappear irretrievably into a crevice
among the fallen rocks.

Espada was onto him in silent, catlike fury, struggling to seize Jaime's weapon and carrying him backward onto broken stone. If there was pain in the arm
which had been struck by Jaime's pistol barrel, the
man seemed insensible to it. His grip was immensely
powerful, his movements quick and efficient. Sharp
stone gouged painfully and Jaime found himself being
forced inexorably toward helplessness.

He realized at once that he was no match for his op-
ponent in any sustained effort and that this man who

called himself Espada probably was proficient in ten modes of bodily punishment for every one he knew, himself. So he had but seconds and he took a desperate calculated risk. Suddenly as though the twisting, merciless strain on his own gun-arm had become insupportable, he slacked his grip and freed the weapon.

Espada eagerly dived for the gun and Jaime exploded, arching his back to drive his belly and the weight across him as high as he could and then snapping back swiftly and jerking his knees to his chest under Espada. He felt his boot heels dig in above Espada's thighs and he used every ounce of strength in saddle-toughened legs to thrust violently upward against that purchase.

Sharp rock cut mercilessly at the straining muscles of his back for that instant, but he felt his heels bite deep into flesh and Espada's legs and lower body flung high as he somersaulted over Jaime, landing hard on his own back. Snapping upright as a smooth continuation of that dangerous thrust, Jaime saw he lacked time to snatch the gun from the now reversed hand still scrabbling for it, so he kicked it away. It skittered off among the rocks and also disappeared.

Espada regained his feet nearly as quickly and leaped in like a cougar to close again. Jaime sidestepped and struck as the man tried to turn. The blow necessarily had little distance to travel, but it was solid, the impact shaking Jaime to the shoulder, and it lifted Espada to his toes. Jaime struck twice more, almost to the same place, and Espada rocked to his heels.

Elation surged in Jaime. At close quarters, where powerful hands and arms could grip and knees could work brutally and superior weight could make itself felt, he was outclassed. But in the Missouri hills of his boyhood, fists and footwork had been his only weapons, and out of necessity he had learned their use, a skill little known among Indians and those raised by them.

Espada regained his balance and charged again, rushing him. Jaime stood his ground this time, shoulders weaving as he feinted aside those dangerous, reaching arms and clutching hands, and he struck twice more with all the snapping speed of his body, sending both blows to the face, now. Blood welled from beneath the stone dust which grimed Espada's features. The man made no sound, but he was hurt, shaken.

He stepped back instinctively and Jaime followed, crowding the advantage now. His arms pistoned in short, staccato drives, almost as fast as the roll of a snare drum. To the body, to keep the reaching arms down, the powerful body away. Over a kidney as an involuntary half-turn exposed it. To the face again. To the vee of the ribs, but always back to the face.

Remembering Helga's face when he had first seen her in Hugo's arms added a special joy to the beating. His hands ached with the mauling they were taking, but he hit deliberately where they would cut. He doubted anyone would ever think his enemy's features handsome again.

Suddenly it was over, the pleasure done. Bleeding from over the eyes, the cheekbones, the nose, the mouth, Espada staggered back against a rock and leaned there, breathing stertorously, hands hanging limply at his sides. It was not in the man's nature to sob, but the whimper of defeat was in his eyes and the sag of his body. Jaime pointed to his horse, up the trail. Espada nodded and staggered off ahead of him.

The man picked up the reins unbidden and continued on up the pitch. At his own horse, Jaime retrieved his rifle and the discharged pistol he had dropped there, and they continued on. At the top of the pitch, Jaime reloaded his weapons and they mounted. Jaime heard riders coming down fast from above and pulled up. Hugo and Helga rounded a turn and hammered on to them.

Jaime saw Helga's quick appraisal that he was all

right and the unforgiving satisfaction welling up in her as she turned her attention to Espada. There was reward for him in that. She returned her attention to Jaime, understanding and gratitude in her eyes. He indicated his prisoner and spoke to the wide-eyed Hugo.

"Tie him in the saddle."

"We saw it from up there," Helga said quietly as the black man moved to obey. "We were almost trapped in the same place. It was terrible. All of them, Jaime, except him?"

"All of them."

"Are you sure?"

"Very."

"Terrible, hell!" Hugo said across the back of Espada's horse. "Smart. Slickest timing I ever seen. No wonder you kept chasing me and the missy on up ahead. Just one thing. If them rocks had let go just a few seconds sooner, they'd have got this bastard, too, and we wouldn't have to mess with him."

"The whole idea," Jaime said. "I wanted him past, alone if possible. I wanted him bad. A present for 'Mana and the boss."

"A present?" Helga's face wrinkled in disgust. "What the hell kind of a present is that?"

"You'll see. When we get home. Let's move."

They were spotted when they came out of the mountains above Mora. The whole crew of the lower ranch rode in escort. Abelardo and the *vaqueros* were agonized in their curiosity, but Jamie held his peace, and Helga and the black man, knowing his nature, held it with him.

More hands joined them as they approached the Corona, so that it was quite a cavalcade as they rode into the yard. Spencer Stanton and 'Mana stood on the great veranda, waiting. Father Frederico was beside them, eyes bright with approval. But it was Jaime's hour and they would not deprive him of it. He ordered Hugo to unlash their prisoner and prod him forward.

"Open his shirt," he said.

The black man did so and grinned with understanding for the first time as he reached out the two packets there. He handed them to Jaime, one of soft old buckskin, the other of carefully folded parchment sheets. Jaime handed them on to Spence Stanton.

"Some old Ute's map of an easy-grade trail through the mountains from the box canyon on the north fork of the Cimarroncito," he said. "That's the way they came when they nailed me and took Helga. Buffalo made it. So can cattle. We'll never find a better way to take stock in and out of the high country for summer grazing."

Stanton looked at the map, nodded, and began unfolding the other packet.

"There's your ranch back, Spence," Jaime said, sounding a little vain in spite of himself. "And Mora, too. The records they cut out of the archives at Santa Fe."

"Obliged, Jaime," Spence Stanton said, his lips not betraying the smile in his eyes. He indicated Espada. "But what the hell am I supposed to do with this carrion?"

Helga stepped forward.

"Jaime says he's a present."

"Send him to Heggie Duncan and Wetzel at Santa Fe. He knows who our enemies there are, who did the planning. And he'll talk. There's three little girls dead at Taos pueblo. Ask Father Frederico. And some dead men in the bottom of the well at the ruins of Turley's mill. He'll talk or hang."

"I like a man who does his job," Spence Stanton said soberly, but with his eyes still dancing. "Come on in and I'll buy a welcome-home drink—for all hands."

"Wait a minute, you men!" 'Mana Stanton protested, moving quickly to Helga Cagle. "Somebody else is welcome home, too. Honey, as far as I'm concerned, you can have anything on this ranch but my husband about now. Name it and it's yours."

"I'll do that for her," Jaime said, moving to Helga's

other side and looking down at her. "A bed, a bath, and the services of Father Frederico, although not necessarily in that order."

'Mana looked expectantly at the girl. Helga smiled and leaned against Jaime, eyes upturning to his grimed, stubbled, and battered face.

"That's it," she said, "and I don't see anything wrong with the order, if it's for two."

# DELL'S
# ACTION-PACKED
# WESTERNS
## Selected Titles

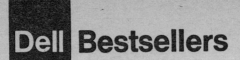
# Dell Bestsellers